# Alive Like Stone

Sarah Pachulicz

# Alive

# Like

# STONE

*Sometimes, Standing Still Is the Fastest Way to Get to Who You Truly Are*

© 2017 Sarah Pachulicz
Autor: Sarah Pachulicz
Coverdesign: Sarah Pachulicz

Verlag: tredition GmbH, Hamburg
ISBN: 978-3-7439-4208-0 (Paperback)
ISBN: 978-3-7439-4209-7 (Hardcover)
ISBN: 978-3-7439-4210-3 (e-Book)
Printed in Germany

Bibliografische Information der Deutschen Nationalbibliothek:
Die Deutsche Nationalbibliothek verzeichnet diese Publikation in
der Deutschen Nationalbibliografie; detaillierte bibliografische
Daten sind im Internet über http://dnb.d-nb.de abrufbar.

# *Contents*

The pine cones on her driveway crunched beneath her tires as she pulled the car into the garage. Another thing she should be doing – sweeping the front of the house, at least just enough so that the contrast to the neighboring houses with their immaculately kept front yards and sterile driveways wouldn't be quite as stark. Yet at the moment, she couldn't even fathom adding one more thing to her to-do list. She felt utterly exhausted from another endless day at work. Carefully she peeked out of her car, looked down the street and to the neighboring houses. Nobody in sight. Good. It wasn't exactly that she disliked people or was afraid of them... sometimes she simply did not want to see or talk to anyone, and especially not when she was tired or in a rush. But the coast seemed to be clear, so she walked quickly to the front door, only stopping briefly to check her mailbox. Wait. What was that? Surprised, she took a closer look. A large, thick, brown padded envelope was waiting for her. She furrowed her brows. She wasn't expecting anything, so where would a thick, sort of lumpy envelope come from? She scanned it for a sender's address, but could not find one. Only her name, Kate Parker, and address.

She became aware that she was still standing in front of the mailbox, holding the strange envelope. Quickly she walked into the house, hung her coat and bag, and then took the envelope into the kitchen to take a closer look.

The address label was hand-written in a beautiful, flowing script, which somehow reminded Kate of the kind of writing she had seen in antique books. There were no other markings on the envelope to indicate its origin. Briefly, she wondered whether it would be safe to open - after all, weren't there reports of attacks on random strangers on the news every day? What if this was a letter bomb? It did have one big lump in the center and felt otherwise empty. But it was also very light, which did not seem to indicate metal of any kind inside. Something told her that his envelope was not meant to be dangerous. Well, at least not in the conventional sense of "dangerous".

She decided to open it. Carefully she undid the clasps and opened the flap. Rather than stick her hand inside, she picked it up by the bottom corners and shook it, to let whatever was inside fall out.

With a soft thud, something small and yellow landed on the kitchen table. Kate could have sworn she had heard an "ouch", but dismissed that thought immediately.

The envelope was now empty. Before her on the table sat a small yellow rubber ducky. What in the world…? she thought. She was puzzled. Why would anyone send her a rubber ducky? She checked the envelope again. No card, no letter, no explanation. Whoever it was must have a very strange sense of humor. Carefully she picked up the rubber ducky and turned it over, trying to see if it had any marks on it that might explain why it was here.

"When you're done examining my bottom, would you kindly set me back down gently?" said a slightly squeaky and rather indignant voice. Startled, Kate set the rubber ducky back down, albeit none too gently. "Ouch", came again. "Seriously, are you always that rude to visitors?"

Kate was too perplexed to answer. She looked around the room as if she was expecting one of her friends to pop out of hiding, yell "surprise" and reveal a prank. But nothing happened. She was alone, except for a small yellow rubber ducky on the table in front of her. A rubber ducky who had just talked to her.

She took a deep breath. OK now, she thought, I've probably been working too much, I've had a long day and I have not slept well. Maybe I am so fatigued I'm starting to see things. She pinched herself. No change of scenery. The rubber ducky blinked her eyes. Great, thought Kate, I'm going crazy.

"No, you're not", said the voice again, this time a little more gently. "Stop acting all confused. I know you've talked to inanimate objects before, it's just that so far, they've not talked back. Guess what, now you have found one that does. It was only a matter of time, I don't see why you are so out of sorts about it. You should be excited!"

Kate stood still and stared. She was not afraid - after all, it would be ridiculous to be afraid of a pint-sized yellow rubber ducky - but now her sense of curiosity awakened. How could the rubber ducky know about her talking to... things? But it was true. When she was little, she had talked to her dolls and believed them to be real. Well-meaning adults had called her a dreamer and told her that she was blessed with a lively imagination, and had explained to her that she would understand one day that dolls are not "real". She had pretended to believe them. That had been more than thirty-five years ago, and she had long since left the dolls behind in favor of a job and adult responsibilities. But even now, as she approached forty, she sometimes could not shake the feeling that a particular tree or rock or other random item was not quite as inanimate and soulless as the world would have her believe. And sometimes she talked to them, as if talking to herself. Just comments here and there, not really ever expecting an answer.

She sat down on the kitchen chair and took a deep breath. "OK, so assuming that I am not going crazy, and that it is perfectly normal to be talking to a rubber ducky and actually get a response... then who sent you? Why are you here?"

Rubber Ducky smiled mysteriously. "That, I am afraid", she said, "I cannot tell you. You wouldn't believe me anyway. But what I can say is this: I know that you feel stuck right now. You are exhausted and trapped, and you wonder what the point of it is. But somewhere very deep inside of you there is a tiny spark - a spark that wants to come out and find the life that you are meant to live. Not this crap that you are doing now because that is what you are supposed to be doing. Let's just say that spark has called me."

Kate was quiet. Then slowly a hint of a smile began to play on her usually tightened lips. And for the very first time in years, she thought that she could indeed sense that little spark of hope again.

Rubber Ducky's words had struck a chord. Yes, she was unhappy. Although that word did not fully capture the essence of how she really felt. She was not unhappy all the time, it was just that there was a nagging feeling of emptiness, of "is this really all there is to life?" From the outside, she seemed to have a good life: a well-paying job, a leadership position, her colleagues and superiors respected her. She had a healthy body, a few select good friends. She was independent, could go wherever she wanted, whenever she wanted. And yet... she felt numb somehow; trapped in the job she did not really enjoy, in a life that did not seem hers. Each day she went through the motions of living, but she did not feel alive.

With that thought, she shook herself a little as if coming out of a dream. Crazy or not, but this rubber ducky seemed to have come into her life for a reason.

In the days following Rubber Ducky's arrival, nothing particularly interesting or noteworthy seemed to happen. Kate continued her routine of going to work in the morning, and coming home in the evening too exhausted for anything but fixing some food and then falling into bed; only to repeat the cycle the next day. Rubber Ducky had found a favorite spot in the kitchen by the sink. From that elevated position, she sometimes voiced opinions or comments on Kate's doings. At first, this had irritated her. Soon, however, she found that she was getting used to and even enjoyed the occasional conversation with Rubber Ducky.

A few weeks after Rubber Ducky's arrival Kate found herself suddenly obsessed with a song she had recently heard: *Loch Lomond*, sung by Peter Hollens. It was originally a Scottish folk song, which he had rearranged and recorded as a multi-track a-capella version. Kate listened to it over and over, sometimes sitting by the light of one candle in the living room, while the wintery gray dusk outside turned into complete darkness. When the candle went out, she often remained in the dark. Something about that haunting melody stirred a longing deep inside her soul. Images of a lake and mountains seemed to form right before her eyes.

"Why don't you go there?" Rubber ducky asked. "I mean, it is a real place, and the song seems to have touched you."

"Don't be absurd", Kate replied. "Just because I happen to like a song does not mean I need to travel to Scotland." But even while she was saying these words, she had felt her heart flutter a little bit. Take a vacation to Scotland? Actually... why not? It wouldn't be only because of the song, of course - that would be silly - but Scotland was supposed to have some gorgeous scenery and to be rich history. And she had not taken a vacation in many years.

With a shrug, she dismissed the idea again. Her time off was usually spent catching up with her friends or tending to the large house and garden; she simply had no time for travel.

And yet, ever since that moment, Kate felt as if something had woken up inside her that would not go back to sleep. "Go to Scotland, go to Scotland..." it whispered, very quietly.

One cold evening at the end of January she sat in her favorite chair and looked at her calendar. She had wanted to make sure she had everything planned well for upcoming events. Travel had not been on her mind at all, but somehow, she found herself looking for stretches of two or three weeks when she might be able to take time off. Stop being silly, she told herself. But her fingers kept scrolling through the calendar almost on their own. To her surprise, there was a two-and-a-half-week window with no must-attend events or urgent appointments, and it was coming up in only three weeks.

"No... I could not." She murmured, as if trying to convince herself.

"Just for the sake of looking, see what you can find", said Rubber Ducky, smiling. Kate nodded absentmindedly.

If she were to go, she would want to explore the country on her own schedule, no guided tours. However, she also wasn't too keen on renting a car with the steering wheel and gear shift on the other side - driving on the left was going to be difficult enough. That meant she would have to take her own car and go by ferry. A quick internet search revealed that there was indeed ferry transfer available for the dates she would be able to go; and she had also found one Airbnb near Loch Lomond, one near Inverness, and a regular B&B near Edinburgh that sounded like a very interesting place.

"Well… now that I've put that much time and effort into finding all these things, it would be a shame to waste it, right?" she said to Rubber Ducky.

"Yep", the answer was quick, and Kate thought she detected a slightly smug note in Rubber Ducky's voice.

Still feeling slightly foolish, but also a little excited, Kate confirmed the arrangements.

The next three weeks flew by. There was paperwork to be finished, luggage to be sorted and organized, clothing to be laundered and packed. Kate had purposely left the itinerary somewhat blank. She had booked five-night stays at the first two places, and three nights at the last one. The first one was on Loch Lomond, because that had been what had called her in the first place. The second was up north in Inverness, because she wanted to see and feel the Highlands. The third place she had booked because the description on the internet had intrigued her: a 'place to just be and nourish the soul'. Apart from that she had made no other plans or bookings for sightseeing, because she wanted the freedom to decide what to do when she got there.

The last evening before departure finally arrived. Everything was packed and prepared, except for the snacks for the road which she would fix in the morning. Rubber Ducky had seemed to regard it as a given that she would come with. Since Kate had no real reason to object, they had come to an understanding that yes, Rubber Ducky could come along, provided she would keep quiet when other people were around.

The cold February rain streamed across the windshield of her car in snaking rivers. The windy gusts and the spray from the cars in front of her had made the drive extremely unpleasant, and the past five hours had been exhausting.

When she finally arrived at the ferry port in Amsterdam, Kate was relieved. She found a spot in the line of cars waiting to go through check-in and customs.

Several minutes passed. Then a half hour, then an hour. Nothing moved. They were still waiting in the check-in line, and her mood matched the weather outside.

Just a few hours earlier, while stacking her suitcase and gear into the car, she had felt the rush of excitement at the beginning of an adventure. She had hummed the traveling song that Frodo had sung when he had left the Shire, and had even gently stroked the roof of her beloved car. "We are going on an adventure, you and I", she had said. "And me, too!" Rubber Ducky had added from her spot on the dashboard.

Now all of that seemed years ago; the excitement had been washed into the ground by the unceasing cold rain. Rubber Ducky had been sitting quietly and patiently on the dashboard, but even for her this was beginning to be tedious. Now she sighed. "How much longer do we have to wait? This line is not moving at all! I'm so bored…"

"I don't know", Kate muttered. Her neck was stiff and her muscles were beginning to cramp from the long hours in the driver's seat. And if she didn't get some decent coffee soon, that slight pucker behind her eyes would turn into a nasty headache.

A sudden movement inside the car in front of her caught her eye. She squinted through the rainy windshield. "Rubber Ducky", she said, "are they… I mean… are they doing what I think they are doing?"

The windows of the Mini Cooper in front of her were beginning to steam up; only the outline of two heads and bodies moving very close together was barely visible.

Jeez, she thought. Guess that is one way to pass the time… but seriously? Right here? Her mood deteriorated further. Suddenly she felt overwhelmed by the sheer size of the ferry right next to her, by the forbidding windy weather, by the lines of cars full of strangers, by the unknown country ahead of her, and by the almost palpable solitude inside her car. What on earth had she gotten herself into?

"Hey", came a small voice from the dashboard. "You're not alone, remember?"

"You're right." She took a deep breath and put the car in gear. The line of cars in front of her had started to move. They were finally being loaded onto the ferry.

Here we go…, she thought.

When the car had been secured deep inside the belly of the ferry, Kate made her way to the cabin. She had booked the cheapest kind possible, which was a bed in a two-person cabin. Back at home, sitting comfortably at her desk, the upgrade to a more spacious single cabin simply had not seemed worth the steep price increase. Now she deeply regretted her choice. Surveying the tiny cabin, she noted that the two beds barely had enough space between them to let one person walk through.

Great, she muttered. I'll be sleeping practically right next to a total stranger. Let's have some medium-sized waves that make the ship take a bit of a roll, and there'll be two of us to one bed. Oh well, can't be helped now.

She began to settle in, which really only meant setting her backpack on the bed and the toiletries onto the shelf in the minuscule bathroom. Then she sat down on the bed and listened to the sounds in the hallway outside her cabin. With each set of footsteps, she prayed for it to please go find a different door.

Time passed and no other person showed up. It was close to departure time, and Kate began to hope that she might have finally caught a bit of luck. She had noted on her way through the ship that it was not fully booked, so maybe there was no one else booked into the cabin with her.

From her small, round window she could see the crew begin preparations for sailing. "Come on, Rubber Ducky", she said. "I desperately need some coffee, and then let's watch from the observation deck when we take off."

Coffee in hand and collar turned up against the blasts of wind, she stood on the outside deck directly above the prow of the ferry. A deafening horn blast sounded and almost startled her into dropping her coffee. Powerful engines began to rumble from somewhere deep below. Crew members were busy pulling in the ropes that held the ferry to the dock. Hardly perceptible at first, the buildings on the shore began to move. The ship was pulling away from the dock and into the canal that led to the open sea.

Kate looked around, expecting almost everyone aboard to be on deck and watch. To her surprise, out of the hundreds of people on the ship, she was the only one out there. Every once in a while, a family or a couple came out, took the obligatory picture, and quickly disappeared again through the heavy steel doors. Probably to sit in the lounge and sip their beer or go to the movies, Kate thought.

The ferry began to roll gently as the waters turned rougher the closer they got to the open sea. The wind was pulling at her hair and howling past with a strength that brought tears to her eyes. And yet, as she stood there with blurred vision and no other sound in her ears but the roar of the wind, it felt as if a heavy cloak that she did not know she had been wearing was slipping off her shoulders. A heavy weight was being lifted from her, slid down and melted into the sea. For the first time in she did not remember how long, she began to feel something akin to freedom.

Before her, the horizon lay hidden in gray mist. Only water, sky, and clouds. Behind her, the land was receding further and further into the distance. She remembered stories of the pilgrims she had read long ago.

Those brave souls who had left their homes hundreds of years ago. Who had headed into the great unknown, likely never to return, to go to the new world. What must it have been like, back then, she mused, to board a ship to take you far behind the horizon? To take a journey without knowing where it will take you, or whether you will even survive it. And the only thing you have is the hope of a new and better beginning.

She felt a kinship to those pilgrims. For her, too, this felt like a new beginning.
The sense of adventure returned. She smiled and breathed deeply the salty, tangy air.
Suddenly she sensed that the feeling of adventure had shifted and had been replaced by a different feeling. It was familiar, yet she had difficulty identifying it at first. With a start, she realized that 'going out on an adventure' had disappeared to make way for 'coming home'. Wait, what? But there was no mistaking it. She felt as if she was going home.

"Well, that's just a tad crazy, don't you think?" she said quietly to Rubber Ducky, who was peeking out of her pocket. "Who knows?" Rubber Ducky replied. "Just go with it. After all, you came here to feel, didn't you? Not to be logical. So stop overthinking already, I thought you wanted to leave that behind as well."

"Good point", Kate conceded. "I don't need to analyze and question everything... such an exhausting habit. And look, the waves are getting a lot bigger. Maybe I am just getting seasick."

Rubber Ducky just looked at her. They both knew that seasickness had nothing to do with it. Silently they went back inside to have dinner and settle in for the night.

# Not-So-Good Night

Kate glanced at the clock. 5:35am. Good grief. She felt as if she hadn't slept a wink. The first few hours after she had lain down, time seemed to have taken on the characteristics of chewing gum, stretching beyond recognition. Every time she had looked at the clock, certain that by now it must be almost morning, only a half hour had passed. She must have drifted off into some semblance of sleep eventually, because the last time she remembered looking at the clock had been at just after 1am.

The plan to 'take the overnight ferry, get some sleep and then continue the journey with a fresh start in the morning' had been just that - no more than a plan. Reality had turned out far more uncomfortable. Between the movement of the ship, the unfamiliar noises and the un-turnoff-able air conditioner, her body had decided that it needed to maintain a state of high alert, just in case. The loud metal banging and scraping noises that had come from down below, and which sounded as if some very large metal object had not been properly fastened and slid from one end of the ferry to the other with the up and down of the waves, had only heightened the sense of unease. Scraping metal is not exactly a reassuring sound when you're somewhere in the middle of the North Sea, she thought.

But scraping or no, they had made it through the night and would be reaching dry land within a few hours. Carefully she maneuvered her stiff and tense body out of the worn and uncomfortable cot and stretched a little to regain some functionality of her limbs.

"Good morning", chirped Rubber Ducky cheerfully from the bedside table.

"What's good about it?" Kate grumbled. "I slept dreadfully, feel like hell and I haven't had coffee yet. If you wish to continue this journey with me and not accidentally find yourself floating in the North Sea, I beg you to hold your cheerfulness at least until after breakfast."

Rubber Ducky bristled and retreated to the far edge of the table. "Alright, alright. Good grief, you are definitely not a morning person, are you?"

"Who would be after a night like this? Just be glad you don't have the same sleep needs as humans do."

After a mediocre, fairly overpriced breakfast in the ferry's restaurant and several mugs of coffee, Kate began to feel human again. She inspected her surroundings. The view from the restaurant windows told her that they must be traveling up the coast of Britain; through the hazy dawn she could see a string of lights far away in the distance.

Apart from those lights, the only other thing visible was dark, green rolling sea all around her. She couldn't shake the feeling that even though the sea seemed relatively peaceful at this moment, there was a mysterious and untamable power underneath the opaque surface.

Yes, she thought, we may have managed to build ships to travel across the oceans, but ultimately, the sea is only indulging us, allowing us to pretend we have conquered her, like a parent will patiently allow a child to play. But she knows that she is mightier than us tiny humans, and that within her lies a power so great, none of us could ever withstand or dream of conquering. And here we are, self-righteous humans, all smug and blissfully ignorant, traveling on the surface of a sea so powerful and so deep we have no idea.

It wasn't until several weeks later that she found out that she had been right in the middle of exactly such a power demonstration without knowing it. That night of her journey had actually been one of the worst storm nights in years, with high winds raging and driving towering waves across the sea; so bad in fact that friends and family had been anxiously watching the news, knowing that she was out there somewhere in the middle of that storm.

Sometimes it is good not to know the magnitude of the storm you're in, until you get through to the other side.

But at that breakfast she did not know any of this. She only knew that her tiredness began to give way to a renewed sense of excitement, as she watched the coastline of Newcastle come closer and closer.

The arrival and getting through customs at Newcastle went smoothly. Kate had worried about driving in left-hand traffic, so she had prepared by watching UK driver's ed videos on YouTube. This had turned out to be an excellent move; the first mile off the ferry proved a veritable obstacle course with five roundabouts linked to one another, interspersed with construction. Although she did not know it yet, but by the end of the journey she would come to appreciate the efficiency and logic of the UK roundabouts and would even feel somewhat comfortable driving in them.

However, at that moment right off the boat she found herself gripping the steering wheel until her knuckles turned white, anxiously hoping she would find the correct lanes, and turn the correct direction without overlooking any vehicles that came out of an unexpected direction.

By the time she reached the next major highway that she could stay on for a hundred miles or so, she was exhausted and drenched in sweat. But so far so good, she had managed. With the help of her GPS, and probably by the grace and patience of the UK drivers she encountered (she was glad for her own car and license plate that clearly marked her as a foreigner), things were going smoothly. The miles steadily rolled past her as she made her way to her first destination. The only thing about that four hour drive she would later remember was the moment on the M74 when she saw the sign 'Welcome to Scotland, Fàilte gu Alba', and the blue and white flags blowing in the wind. From somewhere deep inside, tears had welled up and a wild longing had swept through her.

Her first host's name was Helen, and finding her house presented another challenge. The GPS only seemed to show a random spot by the side of Loch Lomond. When she arrived at that spot, it turned out to be a gorgeous, large manor-style home, with only one flaw: it appeared to be empty.

Kate was tired and hungry, and in no mood to spend a lot of time searching for her place to stay. Unfortunately, her cell phone signal was weak at best, and calling Helen only got the answering machine. Eventually, a text message via Airbnb went through, and Helen was able to send her better directions. She advised Kate to drive over to the Thistle, which, as Kate found out later, was a Pub Helen had bought the year before and now owned and operated together with her son Ian. She promised to meet Kate there and guide her to the house.

At the Thistle, Kate encountered two Scotsmen; one of whom, to her surprise, actually wore a kilt. Up to now she had thought that that was only something for show when tourists were around. It seemed that she had been wrong about that. The kilted man (Ian, as she found out) offered her tea, scones and a comfy place to sit and wait until Helen arrived.

The rest of the late afternoon and evening turned into a blur of getting to the house, settling in with her suitcase and her belongings, and then finally falling asleep in the large and comfortable bed.

The next morning, Kate arrived at the Thistle a few minutes past nine. With a big smile, Helen greeted her from her customary spot behind the bar, then showed her to a table and asked if she wanted a cup of tea. This was the second cup of tea of many more to come in the following weeks. Kate was going to learn to associate the phrase "do you want a cup of tea" with a feeling of warmth, comfort and coming home. Right now, however, all she knew was that she needed to get some caffeine and some food into her system, and then figure out what to do on her first full day in Scotland.

The arrival of the Full Scottish Breakfast pulled Kate out of her planning. Helen set a heaping plate full of food in front of her, and beamed as she watched Kate's eyes widen. "Anyone else going to join me for breakfast?" Kate asked. "Nope, that's full Scottish breakfast for you, dear. Just try it and I'll tell you what it was later." Helen winked and walked back into the kitchen.

Kate took a closer look at the items on her plate. Toast, eggs sunny side up, beans, grilled tomato, slices of ham. So far so good. A wedge of what might be fried dough of some sort. Next to it a large dollop of a brown grainy substance with small darker specks in it. She suspected it might be haggis, but since she had only ever heard of this most mysterious of all Scottish foods but never actually seen it, she was not sure. Then there was a round, very dark brownish-black, inch-thick slice of…something.

By now, her spirit of adventure had at least partially returned, and she decided to try everything. The beans were somewhat bland, more on the sweet side and without salt, so she pushed them off to the side. The brown grainy substance was surprisingly good, so good in fact, that she finished it all. The dark round thing had a similar texture to a very dense baked oatmeal muffin; the taste was somewhat meaty and not unpleasant.

Helen returned and asked how she was getting on. When Kate replied that so far, she thought it was delicious, albeit still way too much food, Helen's face lit up. "Yes", she explained, "that dollop was indeed haggis. We add a little something to make it extra special." Here she winked again. Kate found out later from the chef that the "little something" was a shot or two of whiskey. But hey, it was really good. "The black round something was black pudding", Helen continued, "a kind of blood sausage. And the deep-fried wedge of dough is called tattie scone, or potato scone." "Those were really, really good", said Kate. "Nonetheless, I really won't be able to finish it all..." "Oh don't worry, you've done well. At least this should keep you going for the day." Kate would find out later that Helen had been right. She would not be hungry again until late evening.

Strengthened by the breakfast and eager to explore, Kate and Rubber Ducky set out walking down the road. Helen had suggested they go back towards the house and enter a scenic trail along the mountainside from behind the bus stop. They had considered this, but somehow the opposite direction seemed to be more inviting, and they took off towards the village. After walking along the road for a mile or so, Kate began to doubt her choice.

The narrow path by the side of the road was noisy because of the traffic, and she was in constant danger of being drenched by any oncoming vehicle that turned the deep puddles into instant showers.

However, for the moment, there was no way of getting off this path. It was bordered by either fences or steep mountainside on both sides of the road. She had a choice to go back, or to continue on and hope for an opportunity to turn away from the road and onto some tranquil, peaceful walking path she had envisioned earlier.

The painful realization that up until now, she had been an indoorsy office person who was not used to walking, let alone carrying a backpack at all, hit her with a vengeance. The backpack felt heavy and made her shoulders and neck feel cramped, and the shoes (even though well worn) felt unfamiliar on her feet. She remembered reading the bit in *Lord of the Rings* when Frodo set out, and how he always felt uncomfortable at the beginning of a longer journey. She was feeling the same thing.

Then nagging doubt set in. Why was she even doing this? Would it not be wiser to turn around and just spend the day by the lake? She wasn't a great walker, never had been, and after all, what had she got to prove? But her feet simply disregarded the doubts in her head and kept walking as if possessed by some other will than hers. Eventually she reached a small village by the side of a lake. The snow-capped peaks of the far mountains across Loch Long towered in the distance and were mirrored in the calm water.

Up to this point she had been forced to walk on pavement, and she longed to get up into the hills and feel the real earth and the land under her feet. Suddenly, as if in answer to her thoughts, just a few yards ahead a sign appeared, "Three Lakes Trail", which pointed to a very narrow hedged alleyway that seemed to lead up the hill. She pondered for a moment. If she turned around now, she could easily and safely reach her home again. She wasn't really prepared for an all-day walk, and only had some water, fruit, and nuts with her. She had not seen any maps and had no idea where this trail was heading, or how long it was going to be.

"Well, what are you waiting for? The next train to Paris?" Rubber Ducky squawked.

"Oh shush, it won't be your feet that'll be hurting if this trail goes on for many miles!" Kate quipped back, but in her heart, she had already decided what she was going to do. After all, this was supposed to be an adventure, right? And she could always turn around and walk back if this went on for too long.

Around the bushes and into the narrow lane she turned. She went past a few old buildings and a church, until the asphalt gave way to gravel and then earth. Soon, only a narrow footpath remained. The trail climbed in steep winding ways right up the side of the hill. Then Kate knew that this had been the right decision. With each step, she felt as if she could breathe easier; as if ties and chains were slipping off and she was coming alive.

Slightly out of breath and heart beating - her endurance was nowhere near where she would like it to be- she stopped ever so often to admire the view as she got up higher and higher above the village and the lake. It was breathtaking.

She kept climbing and pausing, taking her time. All thoughts of aching shoulders or feet were gone.

The next turn in the path proved to be particularly steep and difficult to tread, and she had to focus downward to step safely. When she lifted her gaze again, she found herself standing in front of a stone arch with a closed gate. It had a mysterious air about it, and Kate was somehow reluctant to pass through it as if it were just any old gate. Something made her stop and take a closer look.

The arch was made of roughly hewn stones that were set in such a way that the arch was quite deep, giving it the appearance of a tunnel. This illusion was strengthened by the fact that the far side of it sloped downward, making it seem far longer than it really was. Kate felt her heart pound, although this time she knew it was not from the effort of the climb. The path clearly continued on through the gate, and she knew that gates like this were often used to keep sheep from leaving their pastures. There were even instructions posted to "please close the gate". This was definitely a gate people were meant to go through on the trail.

Still, this felt like so much more than just a simple sheep gate. It seemed rather like a passageway; leading to some place or time that could not be seen from where she was standing now.

Out of nowhere she felt, rather than heard, a question being posed: "Are you ready to enter?"

Was she ready? The same place inside of her that had perceived the question now answered: "Yes. I have waited for years, and I am ready."

Heart racing, she stepped into the archway. She could sense a drop in temperature, and things seemed to get just a little darker, only for a moment. The metal gate felt cold but very real to the touch. When she had passed through, it clanged shut behind her with a steely sound. For a brief moment, she had closed her eyes. When she reopened them, everything looked the same. She could still hear the traffic noise and see the village below.

"What did you expect? That you are in a sort of time jump like in the *Outlander* novels? Seriously?" Rubber Ducky sounded amused. But Kate was too preoccupied to care or answer. No, no time jump. But something was different. She felt different. Forgotten was the weight of the backpack or the pain in her feet. All she wanted to do now was walk. Higher. Feel the mountain, breathe the clean air, get away from signs of human life. Higher and higher she went. After a while, the path stopped climbing and instead seemed to take a turn and double back down into the village.

No. That was not what she wanted. She looked around searchingly and glanced up the mountainside next to the path. Right next to where she stood there seemed to be a grassy area which appeared to be less steep than what she had been seeing. Maybe with a bit of luck she could try to walk-climb that way towards the top?

"Are you nuts??" protested Rubber Ducky. "Never leave the marked path on the mountain! No one knows where you are, this is just plain stupid! What if something happens?"

"Well, it doesn't look that dangerous to me," Kate replied. "plus, I really, really want to go up, not back down. And I don't feel like walking for miles and miles just to see if this path maybe leads up the next mountain. I am going up right here."

With that, she turned to the left and began climbing on all fours, grabbing on to tufts of grass to steady herself. After the first fairly steep couple of yards she was able to stop holding on with her hands and even walk upright. Nonetheless, the climb was fare more treacherous than it had appeared from below. Those tufts of grass and reed created an uneven ground that often gave way underneath her feet and threw her off balance. The spring thaw had created invisible swamp-like beds of spongy mosses, and it did not take long before her feet were soaking wet from stepping into standing water hidden beneath the grass. Silently she wondered if she should have listened to Rubber Ducky, but she quickly pushed that thought aside. Truth be told, she felt more free and happy than she had in a very long time. She kept her eyes on the uneven ground in front of her, and slowly made her way up the mountainside. Soon, little clumps of frozen snow began to appear on the ground.

She had reached the snow line! She stopped to look around. The peak was further away than she had thought. She was definitely not going to be able to reach it, and even she could see that it would be very foolish to try with no gear and no preparation. But even so, she felt exhilarated. She was high up above the village and the lake, around her only snow-capped peaks. She felt amazing.

She chose a flat stone to sit on and take a break - not without asking it permission first, of course. You never knew if you hadn't accidentally stumbled upon a faerie home, especially in these parts, and it was not a good idea to simply go sitting on top of their roof.

"You know", said Kate to Rubber Ducky, "I think I finally understand why people go camping out in the wild. Not camping in a van on camping sites with lots of people, but real camping. Going someplace where there are no other humans and no signs of habitation. Just them alone with nature. I'm not sure I can put into words what I mean. But take these mountains here. There is something so majestic and calming and serene about them, that I could just stay here. Just to be. Not do anything but be here and feel. Somehow being in their presence makes me hate the idea that I will have to go back down there to rejoin the human world."

"Yes...", said Rubber Ducky softly. "They do have that effect."

They sat together in silence, hearing only the sound of the wind in the grass. Around them were only small bushes and one lone, weathered and bent tree, and the mountaintops near and far, capped with snow.

"Hm... just as a thought, but what if I was to buy a piece of land here? In the Highlands?" Kate pondered.

"Well", Rubber Ducky replied, then paused. After a while she continued: "I understand where you're coming from. I feel the same way. But you know...you cannot own the highlands. You can be in awe of them, you can respect and revere them, but you cannot own them. And having a house here won't make you any more or less connected to them than you already are. On the contrary, with a house you'd be tied to one place again, and you know what that does to your longing for freedom. You'll feel trapped again, because there are so many other places to visit yet."

Kate was silent for a while. "Let's go back down", she said finally.

Bits and pieces of a dream about traveling still lingered in Kate's mind when she woke up the next morning. Go figure, she thought. She rubbed her eyes. The light was already beginning to filter through the curtains. 6:30am. She had slept for nine hours. Guess the hiking trip did wear me out, she mumbled to herself.

Her brain and body did not seem willing to assume regular functioning mode yet, so she stayed under the covers and let her mind wander.

She could not quite put her finger on it, but something felt off. She should feel rested and eager to start the day, yet she was ...not. She ran a quick mental check through her body. Her head felt stuffy, and could it be that her nose was beginning to itch? Quickly she pushed that thought aside. She wasn't going to get sick now. She had a strong immune system. Hadn't everyone around her gotten sick just before she left, and she had been the only one who had not caught anything? She was determined to keep it that way. Moving from underneath the thick down cover she realized that the room was very hot. Somehow the radiators in this house seemed to have only two settings, "polar cold" or "desert heat", regardless of what she did to the dial.

At least the heat explained the stuffy feeling in her head. As soon as she got some fresh air she'd be okay, she knew. But that still did not explain the odd feeling in her stomach. Hunger? No, not really. It felt more like a bad mood, which she considered strange, given that she was at the start of a wonderful vacation. Maybe it had something to do with the new guests who had arrived last night? She had only met them briefly, and likely would not have any more interaction with them since they would continue their travels that morning. Nonetheless, after having the house mostly to herself all day yesterday, their arrival had seemed like an invasion of space.

"Oh, come on", Rubber Ducky said from the headboard of the bed, "this isn't even your house and your space to be invaded. They are guests just like you are, and Helen can rent out her rooms to whomever she pleases."

"Yes, I know, but I've not had to share a bathroom with someone other than close friends and family since I don't know when. It feels weird."

"Don't be such a prissy. You aren't going to catch anything, and they are not going to lick your toothbrush."

"Oh yeah? Then what about the cat smell and the cat hair that is simply everywhere, including the bed? And the bath and the kitchen could be cleaner."

"It is clean enough. Get over yourself, that is called travel and getting out of your own little box that you've lived in for years. Isn't that what you wanted? Meet other people, see how they live, be part of their lives? What did you expect, that everything looks exactly the way it does in your own little world?"

"Thanks a lot. Not helping. So much for adventure. At least in a nice hotel I could have barricaded myself in my room and not have to see anyone. I am a very private person, I should have known that this wasn't for me!" By now Kate was fuming and feeling desperate at the same time.

Rubber Ducky looked at her, then calmly said: "If you'd stop complaining for a moment, you would figure out what is going on. You came here to feel, didn't you?

And yet, that's the pattern, isn't it? When you feel uncomfortable, you look on the outside for something to blame. So there is cat hair here and other people. And it rubs you the wrong way. Fine, go ahead, keep looking to the outside. Won't get you anywhere though, I promise."

Kate felt the blood rush to her cheeks and was ready to blurt out an angry response, but she stopped. What if Rubber Ducky was right? At least... well, she would be here for another four days, so she had the choice to deal with it or stay stuck in the bad mood and ruin part of her vacation. And that would be no one else's fault but her own.

She sat quietly and took her attention off the smells, the thoughts, and the plans for the day. Instead, she tried to focus inward, in order to figure out what was really going on, the way Rubber Ducky had suggested. There it was, the strange, queasy, and somehow longing feeling. She realized that she knew this feeling, and knew it well. Then it hit her: she was homesick!

Good grief, she thought. Seriously? Here I am, a grown woman, on a two-week vacation. Why would I be homesick? But there it was, without a doubt. She knew this feeling well. In the past, she had done enough traveling and moving between countries all by herself, to have experienced her fair share of homesickness. But all that had been many years ago; the more recent years of settling down, staying mostly in one area, and becoming a responsible, sensible adult with a career and a house had pushed these memories far back into the hidden corners of her mind. Now they had come back, loud and clear.

"There you go", said Rubber Ducky". "Now what are you going to do?"

"I don't know", said Kate. "At least I know what it is now. Funny though, that is the very last thing I would have expected on this journey. I came here because I felt as if something was pulling me, and I wanted to get away from the stress and what felt like a prison back home. And here I am, feeling homesick."

"Yes, but you know, you're not homesick for those things. Only for your own familiar place, your home where you feel safe. I think it is normal to feel like this. Think about it. You are alone in a place where you do not know anyone. You have no idea where your next food is going to come from, or what is going to happen today. That must shake up your system, because humans are designed to want to feel safe and be able to predict and control what is going to happen. With all this uncertainty, your subconscious or ego or whatever you want to call it is acting up and wants you to go straight back to a safe place that you know."

"And since when have you become such a specialist in the human psyche?" Kate did not wait for an answer. At least the 'knowing where the next food is going to come from' could be taken care of. She might feel better after breakfast.

At the pub, only Helen, Ian and the chef were sitting at a table having their morning tea. Since there were no other guests around, they smiled and motioned for her to pull up a chair. They asked how she had slept, and if she wanted breakfast. "Yes please", she said, "I'm hungry." When the food arrived, Kate made a mental note to never, ever tell a Scottish chef again that she was hungry. The plate was piled even higher than the day before, and in addition to everything that had been on there yesterday, it now also had square sausage, a breakfast roll, and fried mushrooms. Helen smiled from ear to ear and commented that obviously the chef thought she needed 'feeding up'. Kate dryly thought that she needed a lot of things but definitely not feeding up. Nonetheless, she was touched. Obviously, they were trying to be kind and were showing they cared in their own way. She picked up her knife and fork and attacked the mountain of food.

In the end, the mountain won. By the time she felt stuffed and could not have put another bite into her mouth, the plate still looked as if she had barely touched it. She felt bad and hoped they didn't think that she did not appreciate it, but there was no way she could eat any more.

As she was finishing, the chef came out to ask how she had liked it and sat down to chat a little bit. Kate smiled inwardly. The morning homesickness lifted a little. This is what she had come for. To simply sit in places like this pub and chat with people. The time-darkened carved wood panels of the bar, the worn leather stools and the tartan curtains seemed to provide a fitting backdrop to their chat. Although "chatting" was maybe not altogether the right expression for the rather one-sided conversation. Apparently, Helen and her gang had decided to treat her as "one of them", which also included using their regular speech pattern and speed. On the one hand, this made her feel welcome and included. On the other hand, it meant that she understood only about half of what was being said. Scottish accent proved to be unintelligible to her at times. Quite often she guessed by the inflection and the glances that they had made a joke and were awaiting her reaction - and she had no idea what exactly had been said and just hoped that a smile and a laugh were the appropriate reactions.

"Why don't you just ask them to repeat it?" asked Rubber Ducky. "I don't know", Kate said. "I feel embarrassed. I don't want to seem stupid, and repeating it kind of spoils the joke."

"Oh, get over yourself", Rubber Ducky said. "You'll seem more stupid if you smile and laugh at the wrong things. Plus, they do know you're a foreigner. That's just your typical "I want to blend in"- thing."

"So what if it is? Now stop psychologizing. You better help me with the plans, I still have no idea what I am going to do today."

As if she had been summoned by that thought, Helen appeared, and Kate questioned her about things to see and do in the area that might interest her.

The exchange with Helen had led to the decision to take a drive over to the west coast and make for Glencoe; which was, according to Helen, one of the most beautiful places in this country and rich in history (but honestly, Kate thought, which square inch of Scotland isn't steeped in history?).

The narrow lake shore road took quite a bit of concentration and focus. To be driving on the left-hand side, in addition to oncoming trucks that seemed to insist on occupying both lanes, and deep puddles that made Kate fear her beloved car might need water skis instead of tires, all made for a very challenging drive. All of that, plus the feeling of homesickness that still lingered on the edges of her consciousness, set her in a funky mood.

The scenery in the mountains was absolutely breathtaking. Despite the fact that there was nothing green, given that it was the tail end of winter, the landscape had a certain barren majesty and independence about it that touched a nerve in her. Something about the emptiness resonated within her. So much so, that she found herself getting angry at other tourists who had stopped at the same lookout parking. A particularly obnoxious group of teenagers who apparently were intent on taking the most ridiculous selfies sent her diving for cover into the safety of her own car. She began to notice Bed&Breakfast signs everywhere. Any and every small village she drove through had a string of them along the main road. Somehow the constant presence of these signs, and the tourists themselves, made her feel very sad. The irony of her own situation put a grim smile on her face. Here she was, a tourist herself, driving through the mountains to see the beauty, chasing some sort of elusive feeling of connection. At the same time, she found the whole tourist business painfully out of place and wrong. As if the majesty of the mountains were being prostituted to throngs of foreigners.

She kept on driving, but by now she found herself unable to appreciate the views. This in turn made her feel as if something was wrong with her. How could she be driving through the Highlands of Scotland, her dream for so long, and now that she was here feel so distant and empty?

She stopped in Glencoe only to get some postcards, without much enthusiasm. Then she continued on the road until she arrived at Oban on the west coast. She found a place to get gas for the car, bought stamps for the postcards and withdrew money from the bank. All of these activities felt as if she was merely running errands - she wanted to get them over and done with quickly, all the while feeling like a failure for not being able to enjoy this trip more. The only time her mood lifted a little bit was when she found a small cafe in a side street of Oban, where she had a slice of delicious shortbread. She had decided to sit outside in the sun, since the weather was comparatively mild. A random stranger passed her by, and in passing, smiled at her and said, "Taking advantage of the no rain? I like your attitude!" Kate smiled back.

Her original plan had been to continue another hour down the coast and then cut across to go back home. Suddenly she felt worn out and tired, and decided to go home for the day.

She drove in silence, just like she had on the way there. She liked silence, it allowed her to think. The constant noise, even background noise such as TV and radio that seemed to be everywhere only exhausted her. But that moment, she suddenly remembered her music and decided to play her 'favorites' play list. When the first notes of the familiar songs filled the emptiness of the car, she could feel some of the tension melt. Why hadn't she thought of that sooner? Music had always been her companion in difficult and lonely times. Memories began to flash in her mind: her lonely seventeen-year-old self far away from home, who had taken comfort in the words of Cat Stevens, when he sang about having to go away because of your own dreams and inner voice.

Yes, she was certainly no stranger to loneliness and isolation. But she had made her way through. And of course, there had been other times as well, good times and connection with other people. Each important time in her life, even each person that had mattered to her, somehow had a song connected. As she listened, the memories made her smile, and she felt grateful for the wonderful experiences and people she had met along the way.

The previous funky mood and lost feeling did not disappear completely, but she began to feel a little more at peace.

Later that evening, she chatted with a good friend of hers at home and told her about the funky mood and the feeling of being lost. The friend said that her description sounded a little bit like someone who had prepared for a big exam. "You have studied, you have worked hard, you have hoped and feared. Then the exam is over, and you have passed. You are there. And then, after the initial euphoria wears off, all of a sudden there is an emptiness. A nothingness. The big thing that had consumed all your waking hours is over.

And you, too, have waited and dreamed and prepared for your journey. Probably even for longer than you realize. Now you are there, and you've had a wonderful start with great people, and a wonderful first hike in the mountain. And now... nothing left to work up to. Emptiness. Nothingness. You know... maybe this is where your journey truly begins."

These words touched Kate deeply. Yes, emptiness. She thought about all the people she knew who, when they went on vacation, packed their schedule as tightly as possible, and who had a checklist of must-see-and-do ready to go. She wondered now if that wasn't simply a way to avoid or escape exactly what she was going through right now. Keeping busy at work, keeping busy on vacation, keeping feelings away.

Weeks ago, when she had planned her own journey, she had not set a program for herself. She had only arranged the places to stay, and had decided to take each day as it came. Secretly, she had hoped for an immediate and lasting connection to the land and the people; possibly some hints that she belonged here, or even that she had lived here in a previous life. Maybe even some mystical revelation with stars and fireworks and trumpets in the background.

She saw these expectations now for what they were - illusions and dreams.

Nope, she had definitely not entered into some mythical fairy tale. Instead, she had opened the door for the emptiness to come in.

Perhaps that was what the homesickness was about. It was the ego's attempt to hold on to the old structure. An attempt to somehow will herself back to familiar places and people, so as to avoid confrontation with uncertainty and nothingness.

But maybe the only way to reach our true inner core is by taking away the layers of outside structures that make up the illusion of who we are, and take a journey inward, into the uncertainty of what we might find, Kate thought.

The next day, Kate woke up feeling refreshed and ready for some walking. Billowing clouds were chasing each other across a brilliant blue sky, promising dry weather and even some sunshine.

By now the breakfast at the Thistle had become routine. She tried to decide where she wanted to go today. This was going to be her last chance for some nice walking or hiking in this area, because tomorrow she would be leaving for Inverness.

As soon as she thought about that, she felt herself slip into the familiar but unwanted 'I have got to make the right decision' - pressure. Only one more day to do this, and her internal performance monitoring system wanted to do the right thing. She rolled her eyes at herself. I guess when you go on vacation, all parts of you come along - even the ones that you'd rather leave behind… such as the 'I have to be perfect' part. She sighed and then considered her options.

She could walk the path she had been on a couple of days ago; she had seen on a map that if she were to continue farther down from where she had been before, she would come across a 500-year-old settlement that sounded like an interesting place to see. However, something about walking the same path twice did not sit well with her. If this was her last day here, she was going to make every minute count and see something new; not go to places she had already seen.

"So much for not being a tourist and not running around to see different things…" Rubber Ducky said in a mocking voice. Kate just shot her a glance.

Another option was to go twenty minutes by car until she reached an entrance point to the West Highland Way, and walk a stretch of that famous trail. As a bonus, she would get to see the north end of Loch Lomond.

In the end, the West Highland Way won. After breakfast, she packed a small backpack and started to drive to the entrance point. By the time she had reached the narrow lake shore road again, she was somewhat annoyed to realize that the argument in her head had not stopped. There was still a voice that complained, "this doesn't feel right, maybe we should have taken the other trail…".

"Oh, come on", she said aloud to herself. "There really is no right decision. I have nowhere to be, really nothing to do, so whatever I decide for the day is just going to be it. And it is going to be fine. So be quiet already."

This helped a little. She continued the drive, reached the parking area, and took off walking. Soon she came to a small bridge that spanned a narrow creek. The creek flowed into Loch Lomond, and this was the last opportunity to cross over to reach the other shore on foot before the lake widened and was only accessible by boat. Just behind the bridge there was a sign, Link to West Highland Way, pointing toward what seemed to be a sheep pasture. Okay... really? They want me to go down there? Well..., she muttered and inspected the ground. When she saw footprints of other boots in the muddy ground, she decided to go for it. The barely visible outline of a path worn by hikers' feet ran along the perimeter of the pasture. The sheep didn't seem to mind her, though Kate was glad that the ones with the very big horns did not approach her.

The path turned from dry to slightly muddy to wet and boggy. Great, she thought. Her earlier indecisiveness and doubts had left her on edge, and now the nagging voice in her mind took the opportunity to pipe up again. "Just turn around. You have not even reached the trail, and your feet are already starting to get wet. What a brilliant idea to attempt part of the West Highland Way in a pair of shoes that are more like trainers than hiking shoes, and without any equipment to speak of. Seriously, just because you walked a few hours the other day, do you think that makes you a hiker? What a rookie. Go home, sit in your rocking chair. That'll be a better place for you."

Kate stopped and looked back to where she had just come from. Maybe that was true. How stupid of her. Suddenly she felt as if her small backpack was loaded with stones and her coat was made of lead.

"Hey, don't give up", Rubber Ducky said gently. "Not yet. Just a little while longer. See where this is going. OK?"

After a few more steps, it appeared that it wasn't going anywhere. The path was flooded, and the only way to get to the gate at the other end of the pasture was to take large detour, that is, unless she wanted to go for an unplanned swim. She gritted her teeth and followed the detour. Finally, as the path neared the gate, it regained at least some walk-ability again and turned onto what looked like the official entry point to the West Highland Way. A large sign displayed some colorful historical information. All right then, she thought, might as well keep going now.

The path behind the entrance was narrow and well-worn. For a while, she simply set one foot in front of the other and continued on the path like a robot. Several times she had to cross small streams of water coming down from the mountains. Some of these had been prepared for crossing with large stepping stones. Others had not, and she had to pick her way carefully.

Slowly, almost imperceptibly, the tension and the feeling of heaviness and self-doubt began to lift. She started to appreciate the fresh air, the way the rays of the sun hit the naked trees and rock formations, and the sound of the birds. Apart from one other solitary hiker who passed her from the opposite direction, she did not meet a soul. Her spirits brightened. Up here, far above the signs of civilization, alone with the trees and the mountains, the feeling of aliveness and connectedness returned. By now, walking felt almost easy and natural, as if her body remembered some ancient tradition. A fleeting image from an old history book came to mind: humans as hunter-gatherers, who spent a large part of the day moving about, walking and collecting the things needed for survival. Being in motion felt good. She kept walking towards the horizon, ready for whatever lay behind it - even though the horizon itself was obscured by the hills and mountains through which the path now wound itself. After she had turned another one of the bends, she looked up and caught her breath: right in front of her, the hills had opened to the view of Loch Lomond. The steely silver gray of the calm water mirrored the clouds. Every once in a while, a sharp white ray of sun made it through the gaps in the clouds and down onto the lake, creating a display of such powerful radiance and beauty, that Kate could only stand and stare.

Yes, she thought. Loch Lomond has called and I have come. I have no idea why, or what else is waiting for me, but this moment is truly magical. She took a break from walking and sat on a small boulder by the side of the path. For a while, she did nothing but sit and look at the Loch, feeling the presence of the water, the mountains, and the sky.

Eventually, the winds that were tearing at her jacket began to feel chilly and uncomfortable. It was time to go back.

She had known when she started out that she would have to turn around eventually and walk back, because this segment of the trail went on for more than 20 miles. She had not given this much thought. But at that moment, as she was standing there looking into the distance, turning and walking back felt just wrong. It felt so contrary to her budding explorer spirit, that it actually took some effort to make her feet start walking back in the direction she had come from.

She made a mental note to herself that next time she went hiking, she would pick a circular trail or someplace with a pick up/drop off, so she would not have to turn around.

Wait, did I really just think that? 'Next time I go hiking'? I don't even like hiking or walking, at least I did not until now. That is just bizarre.

The European tradition of Afternoon Walks was just a silly waste of time to her, and the appeal of walking just for the sake of walking had always eluded her. She preferred a quiet afternoon with a book and a cup of coffee. Now she found that, while those feelings about walking in general had not changed, something else had. This right here, hiking in the mountains with no other people around - now that was a different story. Something about the rhythm of the movement, the careful setting of the feet on the uneven path, the views, the ability to choose your speed, and just letting your

50

thoughts wander until they eventually calmed down intrigued her and began to cast a spell on her. She might just try more of this. Get some decent shoes, some good equipment, and do some longer trips, maybe even camping.

Again, she almost laughed out loud at herself. She, the queen of creature comforts, going on multi-day hiking trips? How about that for an interesting turn of events. But then… why not?

The gate where she had entered the path came into view. With mild astonishment, she noted that her feet had not hurt at all while on the trail. But now, after just a few hundred yards of walking on asphalt, they were painful. Go figure, she thought.

On the drive back home, she thought about her state of mind just a few hours earlier when she had arrived. "See", she said aloud to no one in particular, "it was a good decision. The right one, if you will. Even though the beginning was tough, and I almost gave up. But I didn't. Regardless of the things the critical voices in my head told me. I think I may need to learn to ignore them more often."

In the late afternoon after the hike, Kate went back to the pub. It was a cloudy Monday afternoon in the off-season, there were no other customers. Kate had taken to sitting in a quiet corner during her time off from exploring. She would sip some tea, write, or chat with any of the locals or the staff who cared to join her for a spell. By now, she had met all the employees and had become somewhat familiar with their routine.

When she had settled into her regular spot, she noted with a smile that it had not taken long for her to get used to this place and to feel quite at home. The novelty of the first few days had worn off. As she looked around at the familiar tartan decorations and the oak paneling, an odd feeling crept up on her. It was as if everything she could see was only the surface, a bright and cheery façade that had been put there only for the sake of the customers, and that underneath there was lingering sense of melancholy and resignation.

She thought about the chef, who lived in a tiny room somewhere above the kitchen, who did not own a car and could not afford new glasses. His only pair sported several layers of duct-tape holding the frame with the glass to the side piece. Day in and day out he was in the kitchen; the only way to tell his time off from his time on was by the fact that during time off he was not wearing his hat and apron, and was sitting in front of the bar instead of being in the kitchen. When he sat in front of the bar, he would drink his beer and chat with whoever was working there. Every once in a while, he would get up, walk to the front door, look out the window, make some comment about the weather and walk back to his seat.

Then she thought about Helen, who seemed busier than an energizer bunny, and who was constantly running everywhere and organizing this or that, only stopping briefly to sleep. Secretly Kate had begun to wonder what she was running from. Suddenly the pub, which had only moments before seemed inviting and comfortable with its dark wooden interior, seemed constricting and bleak.

"Have you considered the possibility that this is their chosen lifestyle, and that they are happy here?" asked Rubber Ducky, sensing her mood. "Maybe it is only your perception that makes this seem sad and pointless? I mean, didn't the cook say he spent 20 years in a third world country, where he worked to provide housing and schools to the locals? Do you seriously think he would be staying here if this wasn't his choice? And did not Helen say that she loves being with people, and she bought the pub because she wanted to?"

"I guess... but still. Definitely not something I would want to be doing or where I would want to stay for good."

"Guess what, you're in luck. You don't have to. You get to visit, to experience it for a time, and then leave; all the richer for the experience. And let's be honest here." Rubber Ducky's tone was suddenly serious. "If one of them were to come visit you, and see your life, wouldn't they say the same thing about you? Your favorite hangout is that chair in your living room. Sometimes on weekends the only change of scenery you get is switching from living room to the kitchen. During the week you go to work, run around like crazy all day putting out fires, secretly hating your job, and when you come home at night you are so exhausted that you have to stay seated in your car for several minutes to gather the strength to walk into the house. Then you just barely manage to fix food for the next day and then collapse in your bed." Rubber Ducky paused. "Now. Look at them over there." Kate looked. Ian, Helen, and the chef were standing at the bar, laughing and good-naturedly ribbing each other. The scene seemed peaceful, somehow. From her spot in corner, Kate watched them intently.

"See?" Rubber Ducky continued. "They know they can depend on each other. Helen adores people and enjoys making them feel welcome. She is doing what she loves and lives her life fully. Can you say the same thing about your own life?"

Kate looked down.
"No. No… I can't", she whispered.

The light of day was beginning to fade. The twilight made Loch Lomond appear even more mysterious. Kate looked out of the window from her seat on the bed.

"Come on, let's go outside again", Rubber Ducky said. "Seriously? Remember the long hike we took today? I'm tired and I just got comfy here on the bed." Kate did not at all feel like getting up and going out again.

"I know", begged Rubber Ducky, "but this is our last evening here at Loch Lomond. Look at how beautiful and mysterious it looks. Do you really want to look at it from behind the window pane?"

Kate sighed. "OK, but just for a little bit."

Wrapped in her warm coat and scarf, she walked down the shore and out onto the pier. During the busy tourist season the Lomond Cruise boats docked here to load and unload droves of tourists. Right now, the place was deserted.

In the east, where the sky had begun to turn dark, the first few stars had come out, while in the other direction the snow-capped tip of Ben Lomond looked as if it was bathed in flame by the last rays of the setting sun.

A wave of awe and gratitude washed over her.

She thought of all those times, many weeks ago, when she had listened to the song, *Loch Lomond*, back in her home. She had closed her eyes and wished with all her heart to be there. And now here she was. On a pier that stretched onto the lake, in full view of Ben Lomond. On impulse, she got out her iPhone, put the ear buds in and played that song again.

The haunting melody seemed to weave with the waves that were softly lapping beneath her feet, while Ben Lomond stood on the opposite shore, majestically and timeless. She herself felt timeless at that moment. As if she had always been here and always would be. Her body seemed to disintegrate somehow, and to become one with the stars, the mountains, the lake, and the land.

She did not know for how long she had been standing there, when she suddenly felt her body shiver with cold. Her attention returned to her surroundings. The moonless night was now dark, except for the millions of stars all trying to outshine each other.

Still lost in thought Kate slowly and carefully picked her way back to the house.

The last day at Loch Lomond had arrived. Today was the day Kate was going to drive up through the Highlands to her next host in Inverness.

She woke with a start from a vivid dream. Helen was already up, and the noise from the kitchen must have been what had woken her. Shreds of the dream were still clinging to her consciousness. Something about not being welcome and being late someplace. She felt her mood turn sad and melancholic. The temperature in the room was icy cold; apparently the heat was off in the house again, and she was shivering.

Nonetheless, she quickly threw on some clothes and went into the kitchen to find Helen. It was her 50th birthday, and Kate had gotten a candle and a card for her. When Helen came back into the kitchen from letting the dogs out the back door, Kate lit the candle and sang happy birthday. Helen was surprised and moved; she clearly had not expected that. Then she said she felt a little odd, since she had the morning off. Being the always-on-the-go-energizer-bunny that she was, she had no idea what to do. On a whim, Kate suggested they'd go out for breakfast some place other than the pub. It would be her birthday gift.

Helen's face lit up. Quickly they got ready, and Kate could see that Helen was happy and excited at the prospect. Usually, running the pub took up almost all of her waking hours, and she rarely took the time to go out any more.

They drove to a breakfast place in the neighboring village. Over breakfast they began to share stories of things they had seen and done, from Helen's adventures in the Highlands, to Kate's travels and experiences in different countries. Kate was amazed to discover that even though she and Helen had seemed to have very little in common when seen from the outside, they found they had a very similar outlook on several things. Both had long ago stopped subscribing to any organized religion, but they both embraced the concept of a universal higher power, and they both thought that it was important to appreciate the gifts that you were given. After listening to Helen's story and some of the challenges she had overcome, Kate was deeply moved by the positive outlook she still kept after all she had been through.

After breakfast was done and Helen had dropped Kate at the house to finish her packing, Kate paused for a moment. The low mood of the early morning had passed. Instead, a new feeling of gladness and gratitude had spread inside of her. The joy on Helen's face at the early morning birthday surprise still made her smile, and the memory of the closeness they had shared at breakfast made her feel warm inside.

"Maybe this is what it is about?" she wondered aloud to Rubber Ducky.

"Connecting with people, simply share moments? And in the grand scheme of things, appreciate what you are given, and then be able to let go and let the other person be?"

Over the course of the last few days, Kate and Helen had not shared much time, because Helen had been busy with her pub and Kate had been out and about, exploring the area. She knew that in ordinary life, she probably would not have made an effort to get to know someone like Helen, who appeared on the surface to be much too rushed, and too scattered for Kate's taste. She realized now that she would have missed out on getting to know the truly generous and kind person that lay beneath the rushed surface.

Somehow, in this place and time outside of her ordinary world, a true meeting had been possible despite their differences. And it had only been possible exactly because the circumstances were so fleeting. This was something unfamiliar to Kate.

Kate knew that she tended to cling to things and people, and tried to hold on and control the moment. This often led to her putting enormous amounts of strength and effort into anticipating all possible outcomes, and caused lot of unnecessary worry for things that did not happen in the end anyway. Even though she was aware of that, it was difficult for her to let go. This mornings' experience reminded her again.

What if, instead of wanting the other person to be a certain way, she tried to appreciate them for who they were? And then, instead of holding on to them and wanting things to stay the same, simply let go? That might allow the other person to be who they were, and she herself could be who she was, and that way they might both truly connect.

Appreciating the other person but also allowing them to just be, and to let them go and be free, to return if they chose. So simple a concept, and yet so very difficult to actually do. Our own scars and old patterns too often get in the way, and we lose ourselves in wants and expectations. She promised herself to watch out for her own patterns, and to allow more true connections.

With that, she began to load her bags and suitcases into the car. Just a last quick lunch at the pub, and then it was time to head on up to Inverness.

## Trouble

After lunch, Kate took her leave from her hosts and newfound friends with lots of "nice meeting you" and "come back soon". Had she known just how soon the "come back" would happen, she could have saved herself the tears that were filling her eyes now.

When she could see clearly again, she drove off the parking lot and took the road north towards Crianlarich. The shore road was at times caught between the lake on one side and sheer rock on the other, which made each of the needle pin turns a nerve-wrecking affair.

Kate gripped the steering wheel and did her best to stay as far away from the middle of the road as she could, because experience had already shown her that oncoming trucks seemed to consider the lines a mere suggestion. She had just passed one particularly sharp bend, when an oncoming truck crossed into her lane. She had seen him coming and was able to swerve to avoid him, but that put her off the asphalt and onto the muddy, bumpy loose shoulder by the side of the road. The car bounced, rattled, and shook, but she was able to keep control of it and maneuver it back onto the road. The truck had quickly roared past her, while she was still trying to catch her breath and calm her beating heart. She drove on slowly. Well, she thought after a while, at least there was bit of a shoulder, and we were not sandwiched between the truck and sheer rock. Rubber Ducky said nothing, but Kate could see her little eyes still wide and the feathers, usually smooth, still bristled.

When she looked back at the display, she could see that an engine warning light had come on. Shit. I hope that bit of a bumpy ride didn't damage anything. Suddenly she remembered that that very light had come on once before, four years ago just after she had bought the car. Back then, the whole turbo had had to be replaced.

Slowly she pulled off the road into a parking area and turned the car off, pondering what to do. She was somewhere in the middle of Scotland, with several hours of drive time across the Highlands and deserted areas ahead of her. Of course, her regular repair shop was literally an ocean away.

When you turn a computer off and then on, sometimes that helps resolve the issue. Maybe that goes for a car as well? Hoping for a miracle, she turned the car back on. Indeed, the warning light stayed off. She held her breath. Maybe the bumps had only rattled something, and it was okay now. She decided to give it another go, and continued along the road. Alas, just a few more miles later the warning light came back on, and with it the power was cut. No matter what she did to the gas pedal, the car would not accelerate past 30mph. Damn it. Something seemed seriously broken. No point in continuing the journey north like this.

For lack of other options, she decided to put her flashers on and return to the pub slowly. At least there were people she knew, and who might be able to offer some assistance.

She smiled grimly at their surprised faces when she entered. "Guess I'm back, I changed my mind", she said dryly and then explained what had happened. They were sympathetic; Kate felt that their concern and offers to help calmed her down and she could think clearly again. She began making some phone calls. Luckily her Volkswagen was still covered by the worldwide assistance program, which meant they would send out a mechanic, and if necessary, arrange to have it towed and looked at. And indeed, an hour and a half later, a mechanic from a local shop showed up. He turned the car on, and... no warning light. Everything looked fine. Kate explained that this was exactly what had happened a few hours ago, and that it would come on again. They took the car for a twenty-minute ride; still no problems. It worked perfectly. Kate felt very foolish. Since even the electronic readout of error codes had failed to turn up anything conclusive, the mechanic told her there was nothing more he could do, and the car seemed fine.

Kate knew she should be relieved, but something inside her refused to believe that this truly was the end of the story. She felt it would be very unsafe to drive across the country, over Highland passes and through some very lonely areas, in car that might at any moment lose power again. Regardless, the mechanic shrugged and left.

By now it was too late to be starting the long drive anyway, if she did not want to arrive at her new place in the middle of the night. Even with a definitely functioning car, the road ahead was one she would prefer to travel in daylight.

From behind the bar inside the pub, where she had watched the whole ordeal, Helen now came out. "You know, you could always stay another night. The room isn't booked, and it is still as you left it, I've not had time to change the bedding or anything yet." Kate looked at her gratefully. "Really?" "Of course! Come on, stay another night, on the house. It is getting late now anyway."

Kate accepted the offer with relief.

Now that she had some time on her hands, she decided to drive down to the village, to maybe grab some fruit and snacks for the trip in the morning. She hadn't gone more than 300yards off the parking lot, when the engine light came back on and the car would only crawl, no matter what she did. Jesus Christ, seriously? Why could the car not have performed its little feat with the mechanic still in it? But no, it had waited until he was safely gone again. Thanks a lot. She sighed. I suppose better to have it happen now, than tomorrow when I'm far away from people I know, but…I'm way over this.

Ironically, just then her phone rang. Volkswagen Customer Service, calling to see if the issue had been resolved to her satisfaction.

Given that it had not, they agreed to send someone to tow the car to a shop first thing in the morning.

When she got to the house that evening, it was freezing cold and dark. The internet still wasn't working. Suddenly she felt as if some dark cloud descended upon her. She sat on her bed in the dark, unmoving, paralyzed and feeling numb. A weariness to the bone seemed to grab a hold of her, and she felt tired. So very tired and so very alone. The sound of the waves of Loch Lomond, that yesterday had sounded so friendly and inviting, now only served to deepen the silence and the darkness.

Her brain told her that she should be grateful - nothing bad had happened, she was with people who helped her, who had even offered her a free night's stay, and she had warmth and food. It could have been much worse. Still… she could not shake the frustration. She tossed and turned for a long time, before she finally fell into an uneasy sleep.

Her phone rang at 7am, startling Kate out of a dream. Volkswagen Services, letting her know that the tow truck would be at the pub a few minutes to eight.

She tried to shake the sleepiness, the lingering cold and numbness; repacked the few things she had taken out of the suitcase and made her way back over to the pub. Anxiously she started her car, just to see. Of course, no warning light came on, everything seemed fine. Great, she murmured, each time a mechanic looks at it there is nothing wrong... they'll think me a lunatic.

Just to be sure she took it for another spin to the next village. Still no light, running fine. Almost with a sense of disappointment that there was nothing, she pulled into the parking lot. On a whim, she turned the car off and then on again. There it was, the warning light, and this time another warning light had joined the first one. EPC and check engine were both staring back at her in malignant yellow. Strange to be feeling almost relieved that indicator lights come on, she thought. But there they were, showing at least that there was indeed something wrong and she wasn't making this up. Quickly she snapped a picture of it, just in case she needed proof again.

With nothing else to do but wait for the tow truck, she went inside the pub for one last "full Scottish breakfast", figuring that chances for a meal the rest of the day might be slim; better to get a good start.

Her spirits lifted after she had gotten some food and tea into her system. It promised to be a gorgeous sunny day. Hope began to rise that the car might be fixed soon, or that she might get a rental car and be on her way to Inverness even before lunch, just as she had originally planned to do yesterday.

Eight o'clock came and went, but still, no tow truck.

Eight thirty, then nine. Her hopes of an early start diminished with each passing minute. Finally, the same mechanic that had been there yesterday arrived with his tow truck.

He grinned when he saw her; and to Kate's relief the warning lights were still on when he took another look at the car. He got out his electronic fault reader device, and this time he came up with specific codes that called for the car to be taken in. While he was loading her car onto the truck, Kate said her goodbyes, again, and left.

They headed south on the shore drive along Loch Lomond. Kate could see its waters behind the trees, glistening in the sunshine. No trace of the dark and eerie feeling from last night. Just before she had left the pub to go to bed last night, Rose, a friend of Helen's, had told her: "You know, maybe the Loch does not want to let you go." Kate had just smiled and shrugged, thinking to herself that if that were the case, she wished the Loch would have found a less inconvenient way to make her stay. Now, while she was riding in the truck with time to look at the scenery and letting her thoughts run free, she had the distinct feeling that Rose might have hit fairly near the mark. She sensed somehow that indeed the Loch was not ready to let her go. She shook her head. Crazy. But the sensation remained.

All right, she said inwardly to the Loch. I know you have called me; and it is true that when I heard that song about you I just knew that I had to come. I am here now. But I cannot stay. Not right now. You see, I have a home in another country, and I need to go back.

And I have some traveling yet to do. She paused. Then, almost as an afterthought, she added: I have to leave now. Please let me go. But I promise, I will be back.

As she relaxed into her seat, she had the strange feeling that somehow, she was let go. For now.

The tow truck driver took her to a small repair shop just south of the Loch in Alexandria. As she walked into the reception area, she could not help but think that now she had truly arrived in real Scottish life, far away from fake shiny touristy areas.

She found herself in a tiny gray cinder block room, which was dominated by a waist-high dividing wall in front of the receptionist; and with a short wooden bench marked "sitting area" in the back-right corner. There was barely enough room for one person at a time between the divider and the wall. On the left-hand side, a half-high door allowed access to a small space that was apparently reserved for the mechanics. They kept squeezing in and out, shouting status updates or requests at each other or at the receptionist. The receptionist seemed to endure the constant interruptions, the slamming of the door and the squeaking of its hinges with a stoic and slightly sour expression on her face.

A man in a checkered shirt, who, by his bearing and the way the others deferred to him might be the owner, surveyed the scene from a corner. The tow truck driver explained to him what had happened. The owner nodded and agreed to have someone look at the car right away.

Kate took a seat on the tiny bench in the corner. The door opened again with a squeak; from her vantage point, all she could see was a huge belly that maneuvered itself with surprising agility into the narrow space. Attached to the belly was an old, short man with a kind smile. He clearly appeared quite at home in the place, although he was too well dressed to be one of the mechanics. He asked if she wanted some tea or coffee. Of course, she wanted coffee. Best thing she had heard all day.

When the warmth of the mug of steaming coffee spread through her hands, some of the tension melted. She tried to get comfortable on the wooden plank that called itself a bench, and surveyed her surroundings. How nice of that random stranger to offer her the coffee. This, however, proved to be one of many incidents of this kind. Throughout the day people were offering her and each other tea, and there seemed to be a sense of community, of belonging together, around the place. The mechanics were having fun, they were kidding each other while working and helped each other out. What had at first appeared to be a cold, gray grimy cement building now seemed to be filled with friendliness and warmth. What an odd place for warmth, she thought.

Just then, a blonde, very pretty woman in her mid-twenties with heavy makeup entered the small room. She immediately began to talk to the owner about people and events they both seemed to know; Kate guessed that they knew each other well.

When it became clear that the woman was also going to stay and wait for some work on her car to be finished, Kate scooted over to make some room on the short bench. The owner left to check on something. Kate and the other woman sat next to each other on the bench in silence. Or rather, they were not talking, while the hustle and bustle of the mechanics, the banging of the door, and the receptionist's keyboard provided quite a lively background cacophony. It was that awkward situation in which strangers sit next to each other, being forced too closely into each other's personal space by seating constraints, and each hoping the other might begin to talk or do something to alleviate the growing sense of uncomfortableness. Fortunately, the blonde woman seemed to have no difficulty in talking to strangers, which was an ability Kate herself secretly envied.

The woman began to chat, and after some initial pleasantries about the weather, she inquired about Kate's accent. Very soon they found themselves deeply engaged in a lively conversation about travel, and about language in general, and then about communication or lack thereof between people. The woman told Kate that she had been in an accident, no injuries but damage to both cars, and it had been her fault. She talked about the hard time she had with people making fun of her now, and admitted to her own self-doubts. She explained that at the time of the accident she had been very scared and had cried a lot, but now she had realized that nothing really bad had happened. She even thought that maybe things happen for a reason, and that this incident helped her see and appreciate all the things that were good in her life. Kate in turn talked about her travels, and her current frustration about being delayed here and missing precious vacation days with gorgeous weather. She also shared her feelings of loneliness and of being over-whelmed at having to deal with all this by herself. And yet, despite the gloom, she also saw that because of what had happened, she had met people she would not ordinarily have met, and had experienced kindness un-looked for.

A short while later, one of the mechanics stepped in to tell the woman that her car was done. With big smiles, they said their good-byes and wished each other well. The woman waved at the receptionist and was out the door in a flash.

Still smiling, Kate settled back into her seat. Only then did it occur to her that she did not even know the woman's name.

This has definitely been one of the strangest trips so far, she thought. Random philosophical conversations with strangers in dingy car repair shops... wonder what else the universe has in store for me.

It did not take long for her to find that out. While she had been talking, they had been busy working on her car out in the shop, looking up error codes and trying to find what was wrong. The owner came in to give her an update: apparently there was something wrong with the tupp-ro. Whatever that was, she had no idea. The heavy Scottish accent and the technical language proved too much for her. The owner, seeing the blank look on her face slowed down his speech and tried to put it as simple as he could. "The tupp-ro..." Kate looked at him. He grinned and then spelled it out for her: t-u-r-b-o. Something clicked. Of course! He was talking about the turbo in the engine. Which made sense, given that it had had issues before and it had been the same warning light.

"We're gonna have to take it out and probably replace it", he said. "We can do it, but it isn't going to be quick, couple days, we need to get the parts. Isn't gonna be cheap, either... you're looking at 1600 pounds for parts and labor."

Kate suspected that she must have turned a shade of pale around the nose, because he looked at her sympathetically and then added, "you might try to get VW to cover part of the cost. Being that your car is only a few years old, even if it isn't under warranty any more, but you've had issues with it before. And the turbo is a known weakness in this type of engine that VW uses, they just don't want customers to know about it. You might be able to get them to go in on the cost with you."

He advised her to talk to the VW customer service, which she did. After another 45 minutes of phone calls and waiting, the news seemed even worse: apparently, the towing company had brought her to a place they should not have taken her to, because it was not an authorized VW repair place. Which meant that if she were to have any work done there, not only would she have to cover all of the cost herself with no chance of even partial reimbursement; worse, there might be implications for future claims on her worldwide assistance policy. If she wanted to have any chance at all at reimbursement and keep her VolkswagenAssist status, she would have to have the car moved to an authorized repair shop. That, however, would take even more of her precious time.

A look at the clock told her that it was almost noon. Kate had hoped to be leaving for Inverness no later than 2pm, since she did not really want to drive through the Highland mountains in the dark with a forecast of snow, and even less if she was going to be driving in a rental car with the steering wheel and gear shift on the other side. She wondered whether she was going to have to find a place to spend the night. Disappointment and frustration rose in her. She had been looking forward to Inverness; and to getting to the upper Highlands and meeting her next hosts, one of whom was a native Gaelic speaker. She loved languages and had taught herself some phrases via YouTube before she had left home. All of this seemed to move out of reach before her very eyes. Her brain conjured up scenarios in which she would have to spend the next few days in a cheap hotel and would not be able to reach Inverness at all.

With some effort, she pushed that thought to the side and set herself to making the necessary arrangements to have her car moved.

The same guy who had towed her before arrived shortly thereafter. Third time's a charm, they say, but he did not seem particularly charmed. Kate had understood by now that although he was under contract to take her to a VW repair place, he had taken her to the current place because they had an "understanding" to refer customers to each other.

However, the customer sales rep at VW had caught onto that and, although she had remained pleasant and friendly towards Kate, had indicated that there would be an inquiry. Kate almost felt a little sorry for the mechanic, but then she reminded herself that his action had cost her at least a half day of vacation so far, and caused a lot of extra hassle.

She was even a little sorry to leave the people at this repair place and not be able to give them her business. They had been incredibly helpful and accommodating on a moment's notice; they had given her helpful suggestions on how to proceed with VW to get some of the money back, and, above all, had kept a constant supply of coffee coming her way.

When she made to pay for the labor up to that point, they said "no worries, no charge". Once again, Kate was blown away by the hospitality and friendliness. They had spent more than two hours working on the car or researching parts. In the end, she remembered that there was one last Milka chocolate bar in her suitcase. This she gave to the owner and his team as a thank you, and then said good-bye. She vowed that next time she came to Scotland, she would bring a lot more chocolate along with her. She was not even halfway through her time here, and there had already been so many random encounters of kindness along the way, and people refusing to take money for their help, that she wished she had something more to give than just a thank you.

Another lesson, huh, universe? she murmured. Accepting help and kindness without being able to pay people back. Difficult indeed.

Forty minutes later her car was unloaded at yet another repair shop, although "repair shop" was entirely the wrong description for this immense and magnificent Volkswagen dealership. The main building was a very large, modern, bright, steel-and-glass structure. A spacious hall opened up behind the sliding glass entrance doors. Polished new Volkswagens stood like museum exhibits, guarded by sales clerks behind their desks. A professional receptionist greeted them and directed them to the service area. What a stark contrast to where she had been just an hour before! Hope again began to kindle. Maybe this highly professionalized place would take her car in and get her on the road quickly.

And again, her hopes were crushed.

The friendly repair service rep informed her that they would of course be happy to take a look at the car;

however, the next available time slot was ten days from now. "Oh, and by the way, the cars for hire are all rented out. None available at all, so sorry", she added with an apologetic smile.

Finally, exhaustion and disappointment caught up with Kate. She felt tears well up in her eyes. With one last effort, she willed them not to fall, and tried to consider her options.

Ten days was impossible - the ferry to take her home would be leaving in seven. Would she really have to cancel her trip to Inverness? What was she going to do now?

She felt rather alone and hopeless. In a shaky voice, she explained her full story to the service rep. Her vacation, the scary moment on the lake shore road when the warning light had come on after the near-collision. That she should have been in Inverness by last night, but now was stranded in a foreign country all by herself, and was being sent from repair shop to repair shop.

The woman listened and eventually seemed to take pity on her. She directed Kate to a spacious waiting area with modern black leather sofas, brought her some tea, and said to give her some time, she would see what she could do.

Only a little while later she came back. "I've talked to the guys", she said, "they'll take the car in and run the diagnostics today or tomorrow. Depending on what that turns up, we might have it fixed by Monday." Kate quickly calculated in her head. Today was Wednesday; Monday was still five days off. At least that meant that she would have the car back before the end of her vacation next Wednesday; however, that still did not solve the problem of how to get to Inverness.

Not wanting to appear ungrateful, she thanked the rep, Shannon, profusely. She then asked if Shannon knew of a rental car company close by. She did, and promptly provided Kate with the contact information.

But now she faced another dilemma: her assist coverage included a rental car for up to three days. They had told her on the phone that they would be happy to try and arrange it; they would call again to let her know. When she had asked what time frame they were looking at, they said an hour and a half at least before she would have the details.

It was now three thirty. With an even longer wait, there would be no hope of ever getting up North before dark… if she was ever going to get there. Should she just go and get her own rental car right now, or wait even longer?

The feeling of hollow numbness crept up again. She suddenly found herself incapable of thinking through or deciding anything anymore. She got herself another cup of tea and curled up in the black leather sofa, staring vacantly off into space.

"I know that it really could be worse", she said softly to Rubber Ducky. "Yes, I have to wait, yes, it is annoying; I might lose another day at Inverness, or may not get there at all. And the whole thing might be quite expensive. But then I tell myself that there are people right now working on getting a replacement car for me, and I am sitting here in the warmth with tea, and I still have my health and everything. But Rubber Ducky", she continued in a very low and sad voice, "I am still so frustrated and exhausted and sad. And then I feel guilty for feeling that way, because I know that there are so many people out there who have it far worse than I do, and I am here complaining about nothing but a small glitch in my vacation. Does that make me a horrible person?"

Rubber Ducky looked at her with kind eyes. "I suppose if we keep comparing ourselves to others, there's always someone who has it worse than we do. Just like there is always someone who has it better than we do, which can also make us feel bad. So, either way you look at it, comparing yourself doesn't do you any good. You feel ungrateful if you look at those worse off than you, and you feel small and insufficient if you look at those who are better off. It is nonsense to say, "I shouldn't feel this way or that way", because clearly you do, and fighting or denying that only makes it worse. Everyone has their own life and everyone has their own unique challenges. You feeling bad about someone else's challenges does not help them one bit; nor would denying your own feelings change their lot. This is your life, and you've had a tough couple of days. And you feel frustrated and sad, and that is completely okay. I know it is hard, but try to stop comparing yourself."

Time moved on ever so slowly. Other customers came and went. Finally, Kate's phone rang. It was the rental car company, wanting to pick her up from the dealership and take her to their branch to get her the rental car.

By the time they had arrived, transported her and her luggage to the car park and finished all the paperwork for the car, it was 4:30pm. All hopes of getting to her destination before dark had long since gone.

But by now, Kate was in a state of grim determination. She did not care anymore that the car had the steering wheel and gear shift on the other side and that she had never driven a car like that before. She did not care that she would have to find her way out of Glasgow in an unfamiliar car on unfamiliar streets with rules of traffic she had only just begun to understand. She did not care about narrow mountain roads or hundreds of endless lonely miles. Fear and worry were gone. All that was left was a single-minded tunnel vision that had Inverness at its other end. And she was going to get there tonight, period.

When she finally pulled off the parking lot and into traffic, the rental car felt like a big clunky box, even though its actual size was no bigger than her own car. She found it very difficult to judge the dimensions and keep the correct distance to other cars. Sitting in the far right of the car instead of the left meant that her muscle memory kept trying to get her to move much too far to the left. While that kept her out of the oncoming traffic, it did lead to a couple of unintended run-ins with the curb on the left. Not being able to shift gears quickly didn't help matters; but her left hand was slow to pick up the precise fine motor skills necessary for smooth shifting. Rush hour in Glasgow was just beginning, but she was glad for the stop-and-go traffic. At least it was slow going, which meant it gave her time to figure things out. After about an hour she had gotten through the worst of it and arrived on the highway that was going to be a straight shot up north to Inverness.

There, finally, her internal flood gates opened. She could not even tell any more if these were tears of sadness, joy, disappointment, relief, or even pride. Despite everything, despite all the obstacles that had been thrown in her way, she was on the road. Driving by herself, in an unfamiliar car, into the darkness, and yet she was going on. Everything she had been afraid of had come true. And she was going on anyway and had not been defeated.

Through the tears, she smiled and drove on into the night.

## Another Arrival

Almost as if in a dream the miles and hours went by. Originally, she had planned to stop halfway through the four-hour trip, take a break and get gas. Two hours went by, then two and a half, then three. Darkness enclosed her like a blanket and fatigue crept in. There were no other cars, no lights, no rest stops, and no gas stations. She realized that she had simply assumed there would be rest stops and gas stations along the way. This assumption now proved dangerously wrong. The needle on the gas tank moved precariously towards the empty side. Wistfully Kate thought of her own car, which she had so carefully equipped with some extra fuel in a spare container. However, that car and fuel container were now many miles away. She was all alone on a mountain road, with an almost empty tank of gas and no idea where the next gas station might be.

With a little bit of luck, she might be able to reach Inverness, but it might just as easily not be enough. She did not know this car or its fuel efficiency, and had no desire to gamble on spending the night on the side of the mountain until help could get to her - not to mention the embarrassment this would cause.

She decided to exit the highway at the next sign of a village, and then hope that there was a gas station; and she had better do that soon before she ran so empty that there was nowhere else she could reach.

She breathed a sigh of relief when the next sign indicated a village with a gas station. She turned off the highway - and immediately wondered if she had taken a wrong turn. Had the arrow really pointed this way, or should she have taken the next road? The road she was now on was a narrow, bumpy dirt road, and did not seem to lead to any sort of habitation. What an earth had happened? But the road was too narrow to turn, so she had no choice but to keep going. Damn it, she thought. What did I miss?

Then, through the trees ahead, she saw lights twinkle in the distance. They came closer, and the road turned into paved asphalt again. Never in her life had she been so happy to see the neon lights of a gas station appear in front her; even had the pearly gates of heaven themselves opened up that instant, she probably would not have felt this much joy.

A little while later, with the gas tank filled to the brim, and a cup of coffee equally filled, the last leg of the journey did not seem quite as daunting any more.

Exhausted but relieved she finally pulled into the parking in front of her next hosts' house; thirty-two hours later than originally planned. Too dazed to move, and incredulous that she had finally arrived, she had to sit and collect herself for a moment.

The front door opened. Warm, welcoming light outlined the silhouettes of Frances and Richard, who came out to greet her.

All she remembered of that night was the wonderful friendly welcome, the warmth of the cup of tea that seemed to flow right into body and soul, and then a big soft bed in which she sank into a deep, dreamless sleep.

Kate slept in that morning. When she woke up, she still felt oddly drained and low energy, but that was perhaps not surprising, after a day like yesterday. The weather matched her energy level: everything looked bleak and gray, rain and sleet hit the large windows. This seemed like a wonderful opportunity to spend the day curled up on the couch with some tea and get to know her new hosts.

By the time noon came around, Kate and Richard had covered several topics, from politics to learning languages, especially speaking Gaelic - which Richard was a native speaker of, and Kate found this extremely fascinating. She had a natural knack for picking up languages, and had taught herself some Gaelic phrases prior to arrival.

Despite the wonderfully relaxed and comfortable morning, Kate could not shake the sense of something nagging on her subconscious. After their conversation, Richard had left to run errands. Kate was left alone in the house, feeling she should be doing something as well.

"This is just weird", she said to Rubber Ducky. "I've made it here, finally. I don't have any plans or prior arrangements, no schedule to keep. It is raining like the world is going to end. And yet I feel as if just sitting here is not okay, as if I should be doing something, or as if I am missing out."

"You're right, that is weird. And why do you think that is? Can't you just enjoy sitting here?"

"Apparently not. I feel as if there is some internal manager who says, 'hey, what do you think you are doing? You have traveled all this way to Inverness; within a half hours' drive of you are at least half a dozen historic sites including Loch Ness and Culloden Battlefield, and you are frickin' sitting on this couch not doing anything?"' She sighed. "It feels as if I am wasting my time, as if it is somehow not enough to just be here, enjoy the atmosphere of the house and the people in it." She paused. "Why is it that we only ever feel like we are enough if we are doing things, and simply being feels weird?"

"Well, what is stopping you then?" Rubber Ducky asked. "Go out and do! You've got the whole afternoon yet."

Kate shot her a glance. "In case you have not noticed, I am, unlike you, not made of rubber. Even with my wonderful new jacket I will still get soaked and cold. I'm sorry, the possible benefits of visiting any of those places are far outweighed by the cost."

"Then I ask again, what is the problem? If, logically, you can assign a theoretical cost and benefit to each option, and you decide that you are going with the most beneficial one, then problem solved! Right?"

Kate thought for a moment. Technically, Rubber Ducky was right. She had considered the options, and decided against going out. Why was there still that nagging feeling?

"I guess that I'm already thinking about being back home again and people asking whether I've been to Loch Ness. Then I have to say no I have not, because it rained… that sounds so lame. Then I feel like I have to justify why I did not do this, and my justification is not good enough. Good grief, here we go again… even on vacation there is pressure to perform. You go to certain countries, and people expect you to visit certain places.

If you did not, you've gotta have a good reason why not. I guess what I am struggling with is to listen to my own inner voice without feeling guilty, versus complying with the expectations of others - real or imagined."

"There you have it then. And, I know I've said that before, but... isn't that exactly what you came here for? To begin to feel, and hear your own voice? I've got to say, I find it fascinating how you always maneuver yourself into places where that voice is able to come through, and then you complain when it finally does. Remember the second day at Loch Lomond? You were in such a funk until you figured out that the real journey could only begin at that point precisely because you had no schedule, and because you allowed room for things to resonate with you naturally. Now here we are again. Mastered the car trouble, overcame the challenge, and here comes the funk. So, do you want to keep moping, or do want to do something about it? Or rather, *be* something about it?" Rubber Ducky grinned, clearly pleased with herself.

Kate felt herself calm down a little. The pressure to make that nagging feeling go away had left. Now that she understood some of it, it did not feel overwhelming any more. Be something about it, what a funny way of putting it. But actually... it might work. Instead of trying to push the feeling away, or find something to do in order to forget about it, she could just... be. Feeling and all. Wasn't that what all those self-help anti-stress books were about? Accepting the present moment exactly the way it is?

At precisely that moment the rain stopped and a ray of sunshine found its way into the small garden, making the raindrops on the grass sparkle like a million diamonds. Kate smiled. "No, I'm not going to check off tourist destinations on my list today. But I do feel like taking a little walk", she said.

Along the river Ness they went, getting hit by the occasional raindrop, but it stayed mostly dry. Kate decided to have a look at some of the old churches. Sometimes really old churches felt to her as if the centuries were still trapped between their walls, and as if the whispers of prayers from ages past still echoed among the stones. The first two churches she entered were a disappointment. One had been thoroughly modernized on the inside. The other one looked somewhat older, but something was still off. She sat down in one of the pews to feel the atmosphere. Suddenly she figured out what was bothering her: the noise! There was a constant hum of the heater, blowing warm air into the cavernous space. Certainly, a great comfort for the members of the congregation on cold winter mornings, but to her it completely ruined it. Part of the mystery of old churches was exactly their majestic silence; the kind that made you hush automatically when you entered. The space she found herself in now felt more like an apartment with an over-sized air conditioner, which destroyed any ounce of reverence there might have been.

She had already turned to leave, when, in one alcove, she noticed a statue of an angel. Something about that angel caught her eye. As she approached it, she noticed that it was several feet taller than she was, despite the fact that it was kneeling on one knee. Its face seemed serene, yet beneath the surface the expression also spoke of longing, and that it had known dark and depth of pain. When Kate stood directly in front of it, the angel seemed to lock eyes with her, its gaze gently but

84

unwaveringly looking right into Kate's soul. It suddenly felt to her as if her own longing and pain, which she kept carefully buried deep inside, were now laid bare for this mysterious gentle creature to see. And instead of judgment there was only acceptance and kindness. For a brief moment she understood that this, too, was part of her - no matter how hard she tried to keep it buried.

Then the moment passed. She shook herself as if coming out of a dream and turned to leave the church.

After that she made no more attempts to visit or find anything inside any of the other churches and cathedrals she passed. Instead, she meandered through downtown Inverness, allowing the tide of the crowds to sweep her along in its erratic currents. She listened to the random bits of conversation that caught her ear, or watched people go about their business.

That evening, her inner voice spoke up again, loud and clear. "Let's go to the Standing Stones", it said. The Standing Stones of Callanish. Really? She had briefly looked at them on the internet when planning the journey a few weeks ago, but had decided against them because they were too far away and just too cumbersome to get to. But the inner voice seemed to have other plans. "Remember when we visited Stonehenge?" it said. "We came over that hill and this incredibly powerful feeling just washed over us. What if that happens again? Let's go!"

In the end, Kate found a last-minute flight to leave early the next morning and come back in the evening, which would give her a whole day on the Isle of Lewis. It was a bit expensive, but… this time Kate felt certain that if she did not do it, she would regret it deeply, and not because of other people's questions. This would be her own regret.

When the alarm went off at 5:10am, Kate groaned. What had seemed like a great plan yesterday looked like too much of a hassle in the dark of the early morning. What a stupid idea to fly out to the Stones today, she thought. Whatever has gotten into me? No way I'm leaving this warm bed and head out into the cold.

Then she remembered that she had already paid for the ticket, and with another groan she sat up and shuffled to the bathroom with half-closed eyes.

The splashes of water, tea and breakfast helped to get her system into functioning mode. Her morning slowness however had cost her precious time, causing her to have to rush now to fix a bag lunch and hurriedly scrape the frost off the car windows before taking off to the airport. Now that she had made it this far she did not want to miss the flight.

At just after six o'clock, the pitch-black night was just beginning to turn pale orange above the almost empty streets of Inverness. She was glad to have the roads mostly to herself, because it gave her a chance to practice with the rental car again without worrying about others too much. The small airport and parking were easy to find, and the check-in was easier and quicker than she had anticipated. In her usual "I have to get everything right"- perfectionist mode she had worried whether she was going to be allowed on the plane. For one thing, she didn't have her passport, but only her ID card, and wasn't sure if that was going to be a problem. And second, since she had only booked the night before and didn't have access to a printer, she did not have her boarding card printed, as was advised on the website. But neither turned out to be a problem, and she was through security and in front of the gate in no time.

Coffee in hand, she waited for boarding to begin. Through the floor-to-ceiling windows she could see the small plane waiting on the tarmac, glistening in the rising sun. Finally, a surge of excitement rushed through her. She was really flying to the Outer Hebrides to see the Standing Stones! They were way out there, almost at the west-most end of Scotland and Europe, "next stop America", has her host Frances had said.

Soon she found herself high up in the air, looking down on the snow-capped Highland mountains, the small villages, and farmsteads. She could see the raw, barren landscape. But she could also see where humans had left their mark in the form of telephone lines, farming, or reforestation. She felt torn between sadness for the pure, raw beauty of nature being tainted by the presence of humans, but also realized that most of her own beloved creature comforts such as internet, phone, or electricity, were only possible because humans had encroached upon nature.

The short flight did not leave her much time to ponder these things. After only 30 minutes flight time they arrived at Stornoway Airport on the Isle of Lewis. From there, she would have to cross the Island westbound to get to Callanish. She had read on the internet that there were supposed to be buses running, but the schedules had been somewhat cryptic to a non-local like her.

The information desk at the airport seemed deserted, so she went to buy a bottle of water first and asked the friendly cashier if he knew how to get to the Stones. He explained that yes, there was a bus service, but the buses did run somewhat irregular, especially now in the off-season. Her best bet would be to take a cab into town and then find a bus from there. He even offered to call her a taxi.

Kate hesitated; that sounded like more hassle and time than she was willing to spend. As she looked around the airport, a sign for cheap one-day car rentals caught her eye. She figured that by the time she had paid for the taxi, plus the time she would be spending finding and waiting for buses - not to mention having to get back to the airport eventually - it might be worth spending the few extra pounds. That way she would be flexible and independent to go wherever she wanted.

Lucky for her, the rental company did have a small car available. The only downside was that it did not have GPS, and she had not thought to bring hers. The service clerks provided her with paper maps and assured her that there was no way she could get lost - there would be lots of signs along the way. Given that the island was not that big, Kate figured she would be all right.

She left the airport in her tiny car, armed with loads of good advice and directions from the friendly people at the airport. However, they had told her so many things and had given directions so fast and elaborate, that all the information had gotten jumbled in her head and was practically useless. The same with the maps - they showed details of Stornoway city center, but not how she was to get from the airport to the city center or how to get onto the road she was supposed to be on. The first roundabout she encountered after leaving the airport immediately had her stumped: she had a choice of left or right, and there were no signs whatsoever. Yeah right, she thought, there are signs everywhere and you can't get lost. So much for that. She picked the road to the left, which seemed to head roughly into the direction Stornoway would be. That, however, turned out to be the first of many wrong turns that day. This particular road led her through a small settlement and then narrowed more and more, until it was little more than a dirt path. With a sigh, she stopped in someone's driveway and got out the map. A rather pointless action, since she had no idea where she was, nor any way of determining her location, because there were no visible signs.

A noise next to her car made her look up. A large van had pulled up next to her, and the driver rolled down his window. She must look very obviously lost... but glad for the help she explained where she came from and where she wanted to go. He gave a chuckle and then pointed her in the right direction.

Once she reached what was probably one of the main roads, there were indeed more signs, although she could not decide whether she found that helpful - all signs were written in huge Gaelic letters, with the English translation quite small below. This meant she had to get very close to the sign to be able to read it, then quickly figure out whether what it said applied to her; all the while either slowing way down and being a traffic obstacle to everyone else, or keep going and risk missing the turn because she figured it out too late.

Undaunted by a few more wrong turns - after all, she saw some quite lovely scenery that way - she kept going and eventually arrived at Callanish, where she parked her car at the visitors' center just beneath the hill where the stones were waiting.

When she opened the car door and got out, she was surprised by an odd rushing sensation, as if a giant vacuum cleaner was about to suck all the air out from around her. It took her a moment to get her bearings, and then she realized: what she had felt was a rush of silence. When she had turned off the car and gotten out, there was no other noise except for the wind and the birds. Her ears had found this so unusual that they had mistaken the deep silence for a rush of noise, and had needed a moment to adjust.

After she found her balance again, she started on the short walk up to the top of the hill to the Stones.
She was excited and curious as to what, if anything, she might feel and experience.


When the stones came into full view, she felt - nothing.

Odd.

Many years ago, she had visited Stonehenge. Back then, she hadn't even given any thoughts to what she might feel - she just happened to be in the south of England, and that was simply what one did when in the area: be a good tourist and visit Stonehenge. She had boarded a tour bus along with a crowd of others. Packed like sardines they had been shuttled from the park-and-ride to the monument, and she had been squeezed between the window on her right and the person on her left. As the bus reached the last hilltop and Stonehenge came into view, she was surprised, no, alarmed, when out of nowhere an intense emotion welled up inside her and made tears stream down her cheeks. With no warning and indeed, no idea where that came from or what it was, Kate had been too embarrassed and too busy trying to hide the tears to pay attention to what exactly the feeling was. Later she could only recall it as something extremely powerful and oddly familiar.

That memory had stayed with her over the years, and had finally led her here. All those years ago at Stonehenge, she had been completely unprepared and surprised by this overwhelming feeling. Now, prepared and somewhat expectant, Kate found herself disappointed.

Come on, she tried to tell herself, your expectations were way too high. You wanted something special to happen. Of course it won't, not like this and not when you actually come looking for it. Let's just have a look around and enjoy the place.

It had been just a few minutes after ten o'clock when she arrived. There was one other young couple at the site, but they left quickly. Kate loved the fact that she was alone with the Stones now. She took a couple of deep breaths, tasted the clean, fresh island air, and felt the February sun on her skin. She took her time walking around the Stones, touching them, just letting it all sink in. They appeared surprisingly light, yet not fragile but rather graceful; not hefty and massive like Stonehenge.

The megaliths were arranged in a large circle with one central pillar, next to which apparently a burial site had been added at some point long ago. Outside the circle, more stones were placed to shape a huge cross, with the longest bottom leg of the cross made up of two parallel rows of stones. Almost like an avenue, Kate thought, that leads to the sacrificial place. No. She stopped herself. This does not feel sacrificial. Wait. I am feeling something. I can definitely feel that it is not sacrificial. And yes, there is an energy about this place. But it is…

very difficult to detect. Much more delicate, almost like thin strands of a precious lace. Not as heavy and overpowering as I expected it to be.

With that thought she had reached the lowest point of the cross-shaped avenue and turned to look back towards the ring and the center pillar. Almost as of their own accord her feet began to move and she walked down the middle of the avenue towards the center. She wondered how many women before her had walked this path in ages long past... and what they had walked it for. Had they come here to celebrate? Maybe for a ritual for good harvest or fertility? Or maybe indeed to be sacrificed?

When she had walked around the Stones a good while, she was drawn to a raised mound of earth and boulders some fifty yards away. This mound was really the nose end of a ledge, almost a cliff, which rose slightly before it fell steeply down into a large valley with meadows and lakes. Kate walked towards the mound and climbed to the top. Somehow, she could not shake the feeling that this was actually a place far more powerful than the monument itself. Viewed from here, the Stones seemed no more than a child's toy; miniature blocks that had been stacked in the field. Odd, she thought. Almost as if those builders had said, you know, let's have some fun with this. We're going to build this thing here and fool people thousands of years from now into thinking they have found something really important. But in truth our place of power is that nondescript mound over there. And then they might have chuckled at the thought that no one would ever know. Although, it does seem like a lot of effort for some cosmic joke though. She shrugged and walked down to the visitors' center, got herself some coffee and set out to see the other two sites.

The Callanish Standing Stones were actually a set of three separate monuments, each set on a similar ledge overlooking a valley just as the first one, built within a mile and a half of each other.

Callanish II was a very small circle, reachable only by a dirt path that crossed an empty pasture. The ground was very muddy and full of treacherous puddles; there seemed to be no way to get close to the stones without sinking ankle deep into mud. Kate did not stay long. Off in the distance, on the next ledge, she could see the third circle, which looked to be somewhat larger. Apparently, there had at one time been a path linking the two directly. However, this path now led through a pasture that was currently occupied by a herd of cattle with some fairly impressive horns; one of the massive beasts seemed to take a good look at her and, with a sound that echoed across the valley and sent chills down her spine, began to moo a challenge. Kate was in no mood to take him up on that, so she turned around to take the long way around back on the road.

The third set of stones was smaller than the very first main one, but bigger than the second one she had been to. It was a big circle with four tall stones set inside of it. The four stones were not set in a perfect square, but grouped three facing one. A sign off to the side explained the theory, that this represented the trifold goddess. Kate walked around the stones a little while. She was alone and glad for it; both of the smaller circles were only accessible by very muddy footpath and had no visitors' center, so she figured not very many people bothered to make the effort. Just as before, she felt drawn to the elevated ledge. This particular ledge granted a spectacular view across a valley with a lake at the bottom and mountains in the distance. Above, white clouds were billowing in front of a blue sky, lending a certain theatrical flourish to the scene. The sun had begun to warm the boulders on the ledge, and Kate decided to take her lunch break right there.

"What a wonderful place to sit and rest! Why would people ever be inside instead of out here?" she wondered aloud.

"Now think about that for a second", answered Rubber Ducky, who had been uncharacteristically quiet today. "Yes, it is sunny and gorgeous today, but remember, this is actually highly unusual. I bet you if it were even a tad more overcast, let alone windy or rainy, you'd be running for cover as fast as the next person."

"True enough. But it is gorgeous nonetheless. Can't you almost see the shepherds and drovers of this country, who were out here through the ages with their sheep, day in and day out? For all we know, one of them may have sat in this very spot and overlooked the land and his flock, and felt the wind and the sun on his face just like I am now."

Time seemed to slow down. She felt some of the tension that she hadn't been aware she was still carrying melt slowly away. Earlier while still at the airport she had planned to drive up north to the tip of the island after she was done here; but that required making sure she would have plenty of time to get back to the airport.

Suddenly all of that planning did not seem important any more. She was just going to sit here for as long as she wanted to. But to her dismay, she found that she could not entirely let go of her tension, her planning, and the feeling of unrest, of "having to do something". She suspected that in order to unwind fully and completely, it would take more than a few hours at the Stones; and there would have to be no airplanes to catch or other sightseeing to do. She sighed, finished her lunch, and walked over to the stone circle. It struck her how truly perfectly round the shape seemed to be, despite one missing stone and one stone only half high; apparently broken in ages past.

All of a sudden, the broken stone looked lot like a seat to her, and she felt as if she was being invited to join the circle.

She took a quick look around to make sure that there was really no one else around, because she did feel just a little foolish. Then she reverently stepped inside the circle, said a greeting, and introduced herself to the Stones. It seemed like a fitting thing to do, because they somehow appeared to be aware of her, and strangely alive in a slow, through-the-ages kind of way. She took her place on the broken seat and closed her eyes. It took a long time for her mind to quiet down.

Very slowly, almost unnoticeable at first, a knowing that the Stones were deeply connected with the land and the people arose in her. She somehow knew that the Stones were in a way anchoring the soul of the land and the people. Those that lived here took them for granted, but Kate knew that the power of the stones was woven into the fabric of their lives and their souls. Like fine silvery threads, it permeated everything and stretched across the island and far beyond. Much farther.

She also felt that the essence of these stones was not demanding, or overbearing. Their presence was somehow pure and simple, without forcing anything on anyone. This, in turn, allowed you to bring your own presence into the circle. It felt light, even joyful. Yes, joyful and easy. Like a song of the universe. And healing. The longer she sat, the more she felt as if something inside her, something that had been coiled painfully tense inside of her for years, was slowly uncoiling and releasing. There was no need for fear, or defense any more. There was only joy.

She did not know how long she had been sitting there. Minutes, hours maybe. The sun was already beginning to sink when she made her way back to the parking lot. While she walked, Beethoven's Ode to Joy began to play in her head. She felt that for the very first time she understood, or rather, felt, the true essence of the melody and the words. "Joyful, joyful we adore Thee, Lord of heaven, Lord of love, hearts unfold like flowers before Thee, opening to the sun above. Melt the clouds of sin and sadness, drive the dark of doubt away. Giver of immortal gladness, fill us with the light of day." Beethoven and van Dyke must have felt the essence of the Stones as well.

She passed several strangers on her way, all of whom smiled and waved at her, as if she was someone they knew and were happy to see. How incredibly friendly people are here, she thought. It did not even occur to her that part of that joy she was feeling might be shining through, and could be touching those that she met.

When she reached the parking lot she still had some time left before she had to head back to the airport. She decided to go up the hill to the largest circle again. By now, several other people had made their way up there, so she did not stay near the Stones long, but instead went to sit on the boulders on the ledge. And again, she felt the power of the hill. This time, she felt the playfulness of the monument even more keenly, and from somewhere came the thought: This wasn't meant to be a static monument. This was symbolizing a dance! Truly, each of the stones seemed to have a different shape and even personality: there were short ones, tall ones, fat ones, thin ones, slightly crooked ones, and precocious ones. It was as if she could see the inner circle dance around, and the lines that formed the cross were actually more figures coming towards the dancers to join in the dance. Now she understood the sense of fun and the lightness of the stones that she had felt when she first got there. What a wonderful, joyful place!

Still smiling, she left the mound and headed to the parking lot. On her drive back she took another wrong turn, but somehow that did not really seem to matter. The sense of calm and peace still lingered on.

And to think I almost didn't go, she thought when she pulled into the driveway at home and remembered her early morning grouchiness. I am so very glad I did this.

The weather forecast for the next day had been right for once - it had predicted heavy rains all day, and so it was. Kate did not mind all that much; yesterday's experience was still vivid in her memory and too precious to her to want to push it aside with some other activity, or to overlay it with new impressions.

Instead, she curled up in front of the fireplace and let her thoughts wander. Maybe that is part of the journey as well, she thought. Giving yourself enough time to digest what you have seen, and let the places work their magic. Running from place to place does not allow you to feel anything in the end, except when you are done running, there comes that lingering sense of having missed out on something, but you have no idea what or why.

Richard came into the room an announced that he was going to practice his bagpipes, because he was going to have to play at a funeral on Monday. Kate was curious but also cringed a little inside - the few times she had heard bagpipes, it had sounded squeaky and not at all pleasant; but that had only been on recordings, never live.

When he began to play in the room next door, Kate was surprised that the sound was wholly different from what she had expected. She guessed that recordings must not be able to capture the pipes well, and that microphones only picked up on the undeniably somewhat squeaky melody part. But what was entirely new to her was that in harmony with the low drone of the deep long pipes, a whole new sound emerged that was diffi-

cult to describe and very beautiful. No trace of squeaki-
ness, but instead something almost majestic and timeless
seemed to take shape in the notes of the music. She
found herself strangely moved by the haunting melody
that floated through the house. In an instant, she felt
herself being transported back to the Stones. I can feel
the stillness and presence of the Stones in the sound of
the bagpipes, she thought, astonished. For a very brief
moment, she felt as if she had had a glimpse of the true
soul of this country. Something that reached so deep
into the earth and back in time that it could only rarely
be seen or felt in its music or its ancient sites - but, par-
adoxically, it was still very much alive in its people today, even though they might not be aware of it. Just like
the power of the Stones, it was woven into the very
fabric of their lives.

When Richard had finished playing, Kate stayed in
place to let the memory of the music linger.

Eventually, she got up to make herself some more tea,
and found Frances in the kitchen. They struck up a
conversation about baking, which they found out they
both loved. From there, their talk meandered through a
variety of topics, such as their families, jobs, friends,
dreams they had and worries that were bothering them.

At some point during their talk, they had decided to
bake Glasgow morning rolls together for tomorrow's
brunch (Frances' favorite, but difficult to get in Inverness), and they were laughing and joking while they tried
to get the ingredients to match the original recipe as
closely as possible.

When she went to bed that night, Kate was amazed
again at the wonderful people she had met, who had
been willing to share parts of their lives with her for a

brief while. Each of them had their own story and their own challenges, some of which they chose to share, and some not. And it was okay. Kate was even a little surprised at herself that she could just let it be. She knew that she tended to evaluate, question and judge what someone else had said or done; an annoying habit she recognized but had a hard time letting go of.

That day, she had been able to just let Frances be and do her thing, and simply appreciate what was given to her and shared with her. She realized that she had been a lot less critical and judgmental than usual. Whether it was the fact that she was on vacation, or whether it was the magic of the Stones still working in her she could not tell, and it did not matter.

All that mattered was that that evening, two people who, until three days ago had been perfect strangers, found comfort in sharing their stories. They had found a moment of connection, which was made even more special by the fact that they both knew it would end the next day when Kate would leave to travel to her next host.

In the morning, they had their farewell brunch including the home-baked Glasgow rolls. The house was filled with the wonderful smell of bacon and fresh baked bread. Kate and Frances kept looking through the glass door of the oven, impatiently waiting for the rolls to finish baking like two children waiting for Santa Claus on Christmas morning.

But no matter how wonderful the breakfast was, or how much she would have liked to sit and stay and chat, eventually the time came for Kate to leave. With a heavy heart, she packed her bags and loaded them back into the rental car. It had only been four days, but she felt as if she was leaving dear friends.

I suppose that's the price you pay for sharing part of yourself and allowing yourself to get close to people. It is painful when you have to leave again.

Rubber Ducky just nodded.


At just after one o'clock they were on the road again. The downcast mood soon gave way to the anticipation of her next place. And it was impossible to feel sad on a beautiful, sunny drive through the gorgeous landscape heading south on the A9 through Cairngorms National Park.

She had been particularly looking forward to her last stop on this journey. From the looks of it on the internet, this place seemed like a dream come true. A small bed and breakfast in a beautiful countryside, and the people who were running it were trying their best to manage it as ecologically responsible as possible. She was excited to see it.

The three hours' drive passed quickly and uneventful. The B&B was located so far off the beaten track that the GPS could not find it. However, the owners had provided detailed instructions, which Kate had printed out and followed. Nonetheless, when the road turned into a dirt road and then into no more than a path that seemed to run into a pasture, she did begin to doubt whether she had really come to the right place. The car rumbled and hobbled over grass and stones, but since there was no way to turn, she had no choice but to keep going. Eventually, she saw that yes, she had been on the right track - behind a sudden bend in the path a stone building appeared, which she recognized from the pictures on the internet to be the place she was looking for. She pulled into the parking lot and breathed a sigh of relief. Just then, the front door opened and two tall men came out, smiling at her. Apparently, they had been expecting her. They introduced themselves as Derek and Stanley, the owners of the place, and helped her with the luggage. They said they were just on their way to take a walk around the property, and asked if she would care to join them. Kate welcomed the opportunity to stretch her legs after the long drive and to get a first look at the countryside. From what she could tell so far, the location and the view were indeed stunning.

As they were walking around the property, Derek told her how he had found this place after he had almost given up on finding something that matched what he had envisioned. He had longed to create a refuge, and he told her that when he had made a list of things the future property would have to have, the one thing at the top of this list was that it needed to have a view that would nourish the soul. Property after property had been looked at and rejected, until in a last effort, his daughter had actually found this one. They considered themselves stewards of the land, rather than owners, and had teamed up with several of the local wood and wildlife organizations to design the meadow and woodland areas with trees and plants that had once been indigenous to the land, but because of intensive farming, had been driven off.

On the property, they had dedicated a special area to each four elements: water, air, fire, and earth, to symbolize the deep connection with nature. Each of the areas was chosen because it seemed to have a natural connection to its element: water had a small spring running through it; air was on top of the hill with a gorgeous Chartres Labyrinth; fire was a ring of fire with benches for sitting together. The story Derek told about the earth area particularly moved Kate: One day after they had recently dedicated the earth area, a deer had walked into the yard. That in itself was not unusual; there were deer almost every day. This particular deer, however, had walked slowly and had not appeared to be spooked by humans, as the other ones usually were. It had seemed to be searching for something, and had walked around carefully until it had found the earth spot. There, it had laid itself down - to die. Derek pointed at the skull that was still lying there. "That's it", he said. Kate felt goosebumps on her arms and neck. What an amazing story!

After the walk, she got comfortable with the usual cup of tea in front of the fireplace. Her spirit seemed to soak up the quiet serenity of the house and the property.

Over dinner, Kate told Derek and Stanley a little about her own journeys; not only the current journey through Scotland, but also the winding life path that had finally brought her here. She explained about her disillusionment with her work, the frustrations, and the feelings of imprisonment. How she had felt that there was something out there waiting for her, and she needed to go find it - although she still had no idea what exactly she was looking for. She just knew that where she had been was finished, and something else was coming. Her challenge now seemed to be to allow it to unfold.

They smiled and nodded - this was something they themselves knew very well; their stories had been similar.

After dinner, Derek and Stanley retreated to their own space, and Kate was left to her own devices. At first, this felt a little lost and unfamiliar to her - for the past ten days she had been used to living as part of the family, sitting and talking after dinner, getting to know each other and sharing stories. Now she found herself fighting a feeling of being left out.

"Hey, come on", said Rubber Ducky. "This has nothing to do with you. Remember, that is an entirely different set up. The other two were Airbnb, and those hosts sign up because they are interested in other people and want to give you the opportunity to be part of the family for a while. Of course, then it always depends on what the guests do with that. You've taken them up on it, and become part of the family so to speak. Now, this place here is a regular B&B, a business. They provide food and lodging in a beautiful place as in tune with nature as possible, and they've built their dream. You get to share the space for a while; that's the deal. It has nothing to do with them not being interested in you or anything."

"I know. It just… you know, this place is the most beautiful of the ones I've stayed at. And yet, to me it feels as if something is missing. I know that has to do with my expectations more than anything, because I know they are doing everything they can and they are wonderful hosts. I just wonder if that special part-of-the-family connection with guests is lost once places are run as a business? Or maybe the connection won't even have a chance to develop because I'll only be here for three days instead of almost a week as I was at the other places? Well, it is what it is. No need to over-analyze. I'm just going to enjoy being here, I'll adjust eventually."

She grinned and winked at Rubber Ducky, who just muttered something about "over-thinking" and "ridiculous expectations" below her breath.

The next day was a Monday morning. Finally, it was time for Kate to pick up her car from the repair shop! They had called and told her that it was fixed and ready for pick up, and, best of all, they had not had to replace the entire turbo, only the pressure regulator inside, at a quarter of the cost.

It was another sunny day - almost spooky, she thought. People have told me so much about rain in Scotland... I've had no more than two days of it the entire time.

She dropped off the rental car and went to meet the friendly service rep from last week. When she walked into the building, she thought back to the day she had first come in here. She almost felt as if she was a different person, even though that had been only five days ago. But the Kate that had been there last week had been exhausted and desperate; and things had seemed so dark and hopeless that even this chrome and marble place had had a darkish tint in her memory. She was surprised now at how bright and fresh and friendly everything looked. I guess feeling bad does cloud your vision, literally, she thought.

With a new sense of vigor and happiness she thanked the service rep. She regretted not having any chocolates or other things left to be able to give her, and vowed to send her some chocolate and a thank you card once she got back home. Seeing her beloved car in the parking lot, shiny and sparkly (they had washed and vacuumed it), she felt very grateful. This challenge at least seemed to be over. Nonetheless, it would be quite a while before she could begin a drive anywhere without a worried look at the dash display for warning lights.

That brilliant morning, however, she felt the familiar seat and steering wheel again and was simply glad. Driving now felt easy, and she thought that she was getting to be quite good at the "other-side"-driving. "Interesting", she said to Rubber Ducky. "Had I been driving in my own car all this time, I'm not sure I would by now be thinking of the driving here as easy. But because the universe had raised the bar and given me something much more difficult to deal with, now the step down seems super easy. Wonder if there is a lesson in that as well…"

Feeling ready for some driving and adventure, Kate decided to go see the ruins of the cathedral in St. Andrews. This had been one of the things that she had really want to see yet, and today seemed like a perfect opportunity.

When the sign "Welcome to St. Andrews" appeared after a two-hour drive, Kate was surprised. She had expected a bigger city, but this seemed almost rural. Maybe she had pointed the GPS to the wrong St. Andrews? Or these were the way-outer-outskirts? But no, it was the right St. Andrews. It did become a little more town-y, and as she drove into the center it became even city-like. Nonetheless, she thought it quaint and charming. However, she was glad to have her own car again to navigate the tiny alleyways in search of parking near the cathedral.

Again, her expectations had been completely off. She had only seen a few pictures, and had envisioned a cathedral that stood somewhat isolated with ample space, even lawns around it. The reality was that the city seemed to be encroaching on the old cathedral; the thin stone wall that surrounded it seemed to only barely be able to stem the oncoming tide of newer stone buildings. And there was nowhere else to go, for this cathedral, too, was built on a cliff that overlooked the sea. Another ancient place on a hill near a cliff... What was it about places like this that drew people back then? Kate wondered.

She entered the enclosed area through an iron gate. Even though it was almost midday, the February sun had not quite been able to lift all of the fog that had come in from the sea. The ruinous walls and spires loomed through shrouds of fog, and the gloom that was cast by large banks of clouds gave an eerie appearance to the scene in front of her. Grave stones, large crosses and angel statues crowded around the stony outline of where the cathedral had once been. The place had a mysterious and somehow very sad feeling to it.

Kate wandered among the graves and around what was left of the cathedral walls.

"This place makes me feel the decay and ephemeral nature of things so much more than the Stones of Callanish, even though the Stones are far older", she said to Rubber Ducky. "Just think, this is a place that was the largest church to have been built in this country; the seat of all religious power at the time. It must have been incredibly grand and splendid, full of life, and full of people coming and going. Now, about 800 years later, all that's left of it are these two crumbling walls and a tower, and an outline on the ground of where the walls used to be. These walls seem to decay before your very eyes, and instead of clergy and peasants coming and going, there are only crowds of tourists or busloads of Scottish school children on a field trip to learn their country's history. It's kind of sad, isn't it?"

Rubber Ducky made no reply, but she seemed equally moved by the deep melancholy that seemed to hang between the remnants of the walls like the sea fog.

Apart from Kate, several other tourists were roaming about the place. She guessed that in the summer, there would be huge crowds spilling in through the narrow gates like water through a floodgate. But even the few that walked around now seemed out of place. It felt strangely similar to sitting at a viewing of a dead body, with oblivious strangers walking in and out, looking at the coffin as if it were an item on display in a store.

Built into one of the decaying walls there were many small alcoves, just big enough for one person to sit inside on the built-in small shelf. The illustration on a sign nearby showed that this really had been where clergymen had sat during worship or probably during meetings as well. She took a seat in one of them. It seemed a strange thing to imagine that a thousand years ago, someone had sat in exactly this spot, and had felt these same cool and slightly rough stones in his back. Instead of the green grass and the sky overhead he would have seen artistically laid stone flooring, decorated pillars, and sweeping ceilings high above. The sounds would not have been wind and waves, but the chatter of his fellow clergymen, or the chanting of the liturgy. She closed her eyes.

A little while later she opened them again, showing a puzzled expression.

Hm. This place here had been a place of worship for several hundred years, complete with relics of saints and all. Now, I would have expected to have a similar sense of reverence and - well - holiness, so to speak, as I did at the Stones, or in some of the other old churches that I've been in. But I don't.

She found that it was difficult to put into words what she had sensed. She thought, it is very faint anymore; really it is mostly about the decay and the endedness. But there is something there, not sacred though. Rather, it feels like worldly power. Masculine, almost... strategic. How bizarre. No, she corrected herself, not bizarre if you think about it. After all, there probably had been a good bit of scheming and strategizing among these walls, and more than likely, most of it motivated by desires other than faith or humility. But still… Her thoughts trailed off and were lost again in the depth of time.

By now, the afternoon had become bright and sunny, and it seemed as if spring was just around the corner. Her grumbling stomach reminded her that it had been a good many hours since breakfast. She took a stroll through downtown St. Andrews, which was beautiful and charming, and found some food to calm her stomach. The mysterious atmosphere of the cathedral still occupied her mind, and she felt that it was time to drive back to the B&B. Long car drives always helped her think and sort things out; and after another coffee from a very cute coffee shop in one of the side alleys, she was on her way.

This was the last full day in Scotland. Tomorrow, Kate would be boarding the ferry and head back home. Quickly she pushed that thought aside. She still had today, and she was going to make it count. She wanted to feel the earth, the land under her feet. To the north of the B&B there was a hill, the top of which, from what Stanley had told her, could be reached in about an hours' time.

The idea of some light hiking and the prospect of a great view of the countryside made this sound like an excellent choice to spend the day. The sky was somewhat overcast, but it did not look like rain anytime soon. After another wonderful breakfast, Kate set off in the direction of the hill just after 10am.

Soon she had reached the foot of the hill. From a distance, it had looked quite small, but now, from directly below, it appeared very high, steep, and looming.

Kate adjusted her backpack and began the ascent. At first, there was even a road of sorts, which led to a quarry. From there, she had to go through a gate and then follow a muddy dirt path to go further up. Eventually, the path got narrower and narrower, until it disappeared into the grass. Kate looked up and discovered that she was very nearly at the top already. Just maybe twenty or thirty yards of steep grassy incline and she would be there. Slowly, methodically she walked up the incline, sometimes holding on with her hands as well, being careful to keep her balance. She began to breathe faster and felt her heart beat. Quite a workout, she thought. So much for 'easy hike', thanks Stanley! Just when she thought her leg muscles would need a break, the incline began to level off. She must have made it! She straightened up and took a look around to enjoy the view.

But - what was that? No way. There, right in front of her, the hill continued to loom and rise up even higher. Apparently, she had only reached a plateau on the hillside, which must have obscured the view to the actual hilltop from below. Seriously? she grumbled. Briefly the thought of simply stopping there crossed her mind. But no, that wasn't even an option. Of course she was going to reach the top.

Even from where she was now, the view was already breathtaking. A slight haze softened the contours of distant hills and woods, while the occasional ray of sun highlighted a field or a group of trees.

After catching her breath, she continued to move up. She estimated that she had already come two thirds of the way up. Moving ahead slowly and carefully, feeling a little bit as if she was an ant crawling up the side of a giant anthill, she continued to walk, climb, or truly crawl. It took all of her focus to keep her balance, and she did not look up again until this incline, too, began to level off.

With a sigh of relief, she stretched her back. This last effort had taken almost all her strength. Then she lifted her gaze from the ground, only to see that she had - again - not reached the top. This appeared to be a shoulder on the side of the hill, with the real top set back a couple of hundred yards and rising yet again.

"Damn", she said, out of breath and frustrated. "That is just not fair…"

"It is a little bit like in real life, isn't it?" Rubber Ducky responded. "You set out to climb a hill, and then when you think you've reached the top, you find out that really you've only come to the first stage. So you gather your energy, set your sights on your goal again, and plod along. You think you've finally got there, only to see that the goal seems to have moved. But by now you've mobilized almost all your energy for that last effort because you thought that would be it. And now you have to decide what to do - keep going or abandon the quest?"

But there was no abandoning anything. Ambition drove Kate now, and she would keep going, regardless. Rubber Ducky smiled to herself. "Yep, just like in real life", she said with only a hint of sarcasm in her voice. But Kate only shot her a sideways glance.

She had to cross a sheep pasture again; those horns were still impressive but fortunately the sheep kept their distance. Then the slope increased again. Now for the last ascent, for real this time. The wind tore at her clothes and made her eyes water. She was glad for the windproof jacket and ear protection she had. After all, it was technically still winter.

After another seemingly endless stretch of walking and partially crawling, she reached the top. The actual, real top. She stood still for a moment, breathing hard, waiting for the disbelief that she had actually made it to subside. Then, she felt a wave of joy and pride. She had made it!

The view was stunning; she could see the green rolling hills all around and the mountains in the distance. To the other side, the bay of Forth, which lead to the sea, glittered in the sun. She breathed deeply and enjoyed just being there. However, the wind and chill temperatures did not allow her to stay up there long. Very soon she felt compelled to walk back down the side of the hill to seek at least some shelter from the icy gusts.

Well, she mused, so that was it, hm? You make it, you finally reach the top, you admire the view, and then you wonder, now what? What else is there to do? "I think, Rubber Ducky", she said, "maybe I understand a little bit more of what people mean when they say, 'it is about the journey, not about the destination'. You know, while you're climbing up, at least you still have something to do, you have a purpose. And even when you find that there is yet more to climb, although you thought you were done - you learn to deal with the frustration and you keep going anyway. You keep going, through fatigue and aching muscles, simply because you have somewhere to go. You have a goal: the top. And then…" her voice turned low and somehow sad, "… once you have reached the top, there is nowhere else to go. At least not up higher. Only back down."

"Yes, that is true", Rubber Ducky said. "So, you think climbing hills is pointless and you won't do it again?"

"Oh no, that is not what I meant at all", Kate said quickly. "I mean, I think it has both. The bitter and the sweet. I would not trade this experience for the world, and I would do it again… maybe not this hill, but other hills for sure. No", she said after a brief pause, "probably not this one again. That definitely has a "been there, done that" quality now. But no, the fact that in the end you have to go back down again would not stop me from going up in the first place. That would be like saying 'never try anything, because in the end you'll be back at home anyway so you may as well never leave!' That would not do at all! At least not for me. Maybe going out and climbing hills requires effort and is uncomfortable and lonely at times. But the freedom and the sense of accomplishment I get from it more than make up for it. Besides… there are so many hills and mountains out there, only waiting for me to climb them!" She smiled. Then, slowly and carefully, through the icy wind and steep, uneven ground, she made her way back down the hill.

The cold and the wind had chilled her to the bone. She thought of the big bathtub in her bathroom, and the idea of a nice hot bubble bath seemed heavenly. Soon after she got back she had the hot water running. The soap filled the bath with bubbles and refreshed the air with a lovely citrus scent.

She left the tub to fill while she went back to her room to peel out of her sweaty clothes, put on the bath robe that had been provided, and to invite Rubber Ducky to come with. "Are you kidding me? It's a bubble bath, why do you even ask?"

Kate smiled, rolled her eyes a little and returned to the bathroom. She checked the temperature of the water and froze, literally. The running water that came out of the tap was cold. Ice cold. She put her hand into the water in the tub. Warm. Luke warm. "No no no no, please..." she murmured. "Please don't run out of hot water now, when I'm cold and tired and sore and the only thing I want to do is take a hot bath! Please??"

She tried the sink. Cold water as well. Yup... she had no idea how the boiler system or hot water tanks were set up in this house, but clearly there did not seem to be any more hot water forthcoming at this moment.

Shivering slightly in her thin bathrobe, she stood in front of the bathtub and debated what to do. She really needed a rinse of some sort. Given that the shower was going to be icy, maybe the bath water was at least somewhat acceptable? She felt the temperature of the water again. Definitely not hot, but not super-cold either. She might give it a try.

Carefully she slid into the tub. The water was barely enough to cover her. She tried to relax and pretend that she was in a hot bath. No... it was no use. The water had exactly that temperature at one or two degrees below body temperature, which made it feel sort of warm to the skin but quickly made one feel cold inside. This was useless. After a quick basic rinse, she got out of the tub, still cold and shivering even harder.

All the while, Rubber Ducky had been happily swimming around in the water. "At least one of us is enjoying herself", Kate said grimly through chattering teeth. She took Rubber Ducky out of the tub and set her on the rim to dry, while she toweled herself off vigorously in an attempt to regain some warmth.

Well, if there isn't any hot water to be had, maybe at least some hot coffee, or tea, or whatever. Anything hot, she thought. She wrapped herself into her bathrobe and unlocked the bathroom door. That is, she tried. With disbelief and horror, she stared at the door lock, where the knob that was used to turn and open it had just come off into her hand. Gently she tried the handle. Nope, still locked. For a moment, time seemed to have stopped, while her brain still refused to process the information from her eyes and hand. She breathed deeply and tried the handle again. The door did not budge. The golden knob was still in her hand. On the door, where it used to be, there was now a hole through which a square bolt was visible. Clearly, that bolt needed to be turned to retract the latch that currently locked the door to the frame. She tried to put the knob back into place, but it would not slide back onto the square bolt. The bolt must have shifted backwards, and the knob was now useless.

When it became clear that the door was definitely and truly locked, and there was no immediately apparent way to open it, the full extent of her predicament hit her. She was locked in a bathroom at the end of a hallway on the first floor of a very large house. She had no idea if there was even anyone still in the house, or if they had all gone out to run errands or work in the garden. And nobody knew where she was or what her plans had been for the day, so they would not be missing her for at least another four to five hours. Even if she did not show up for dinner, they might just assume she had eaten somewhere else and would not suspect anything wrong or come looking for her.

If she wanted out of this place anytime soon she would either have to find a way out, or make a lot of noise in the dim hope that someone might be in the vicinity and hear her.

She felt oddly surreal, as if a part of her was watching herself from above: a small helpless human trapped in a cage and trying desperately to find a way out. This was not really happening, was it? Things like this only happened in soap operas or comedy shows, and people laughed and it was funny. This definitely felt about as far away from funny as she ever had.

Suddenly she heard a noise and a splash behind her. Rubber Ducky for her part had apparently thought the situation very funny, and she had laughed so hard that she had lost her balance and fallen back into the tub.
"Lucky you that there was still water in the tub, or you'd have broken your neck, and it would have served you right!" Kate hissed angrily. But this was the little push she had needed to move into action and problem-

solving mode. Looking at Rubber Ducky and the rim of the tub where she had sat a moment ago gave her an idea. The rooftop window was right above the tub. If she climbed onto the rim and stood on it, she would be able to open the window and see out. Maybe there was a way to climb out, or maybe she could see someone in the yard and call for help.

Carefully she stepped onto the rim and pulled herself up. Don't need to be slipping and breaking anything on top of this, she told herself. However, the view from the window proved a disappointment. No other person in sight. The roof all around the window sloped very steeply down until it reached the lower, more level roof above the sun porch. Even if she were able to manage to pull herself up and out of the window frame, and then somehow slide down the steep incline and land on the flat roof of the porch (that feat alone would require more acrobatic abilities than she had ever possessed), she would still have to maneuver her whole body over the edge of the lower roof until she hung on only by her hands, and then let go and jump down to the bottom. And of course, the whole stunt would have to be done while being clad only in a flimsy bathrobe, which likely would provide no cover whatsoever by the time she got to hang from the side of the sun porch. Nope, not going to happen, she said to herself. "And don't even think about some smart-ass comment now!" she said to Rubber Ducky, who had indeed just opened her beak. But she quickly closed it again, sensing that it might be good to stop wisecracking for a while. After all, she did want to travel back home with Kate and not be left behind.

With possible alternative escape routes ruled out, Kate turned her attention back to the door and the lock. Was there any way she could still turn the bolt inside the door? She could not reach it with her fingers, but maybe some other utensil… an idea struck her, and she rummaged in her toiletries bag, which she had fortunately placed here in the bathroom. Maybe there was something here? The search turned up a hairpin, tweezers, and a nail file as possible candidates for lock picking.

The tweezers looked promising; they actually fit in the narrow space inside the hole and she was able to grasp the square bolt with them. With all her might she squeezed them like pliers and turned. Nothing. The bolt did not budge even a hair's breadth. The only thing that took a turn for the worse were the tweezers - they were clearly much too delicate for a job like this and started to bend under the pressure. Trying to reinforce them with the nail file, or using the nail file and tweezers in unison did not work, either. The last, desperate attempt finally led to the bolt popping out on the other side of the door and landing with a thud on the floor. Now any hope of manipulating the lock was gone.

Kate sat down on the rim of the bathtub and took a breath. All thoughts of freezing or cold had vanished; on the contrary, she felt very flushed. "Well", said Rubber Ducky, trying to sound sympathetic. Secretly she still thought the whole situation absolutely hilarious, but she sensed that Kate was in no mood to joke and was actually quite tense. "I guess there's nothing else but trying to raise someone's attention by making as much noise as you can."

"Guess you are right", said Kate. Oh boy, this was so embarrassing. Again, she felt as if a hidden camera might pop out any minute and some cheerful TV host with a big fake smile might come around a corner. But no such luck. There was nothing else to do, so she began to pound her fists against the bathroom doors, stopping every so often to listen for sounds from outside, or to cry for help through the hole in the door where the lock had once been.

It felt as if an eternity had passed, but in reality, it probably had not been more than five or ten minutes, when she suddenly heard footsteps on the landing and Derek's voice yelling, "coming!" A few seconds later she could hear him by the door, and there was a note of bewilderment in his voice when he said, "gee, I see the lock has completely come out. Hold on." She could hear him picking up the counterpart to her turning knob, and tell her to fit hers into its place. With the pressure he provided on the other side, the knob was fitted onto the bolt again, and she was able to turn the lock. The door opened.

So great was the relief that at that moment she did not care about not wearing anything but a flimsy bathrobe. Derek looked at her with a concerned expression and asked if she was okay. She managed to say yes, although her knees were beginning to feel increasingly like pudding.

Quickly she assured him that she was fine. When he had left to find tools to repair the door, she willed her pudding legs to take her back to her room. With some effort, she got dressed and then sat down in the chair.

She took several deep breaths.

All things considered, she had been lucky... it had not taken very long to be rescued, and nothing really bad had happened. Still, she felt a little shaky.

Now that she was back in the comfort of her room, suddenly a surge of anger came out of nowhere. Anger at Derek, that all he had done was to ask, "are you okay" and then leave. A bit more empathy, such as an "oh dear, that must have been scary, come let me make you a cup of tea" would have been nice. Or was that her own unrealistic expectations again? She began to doubt herself, and anger was replaced with loneliness. She suspected that her system was simply a bit shaken up by the excitement.

"It probably is", said Rubber Ducky. In her best teacher voice, she continued: "While you were locked in there, your body switched to emergency state, and tried to ensure your survival. Nothing else matters at a time like that. But when that is over, and the body goes back into regular mode, your attachment system bounces back full force. It seeks the comfort of others, which helps to regulate your out-of-whack system. You are wired that way. But given that none of your friends were at hand, the next people in line were Derek and Stanley. From Derek's perspective, he did everything right: rescued you, asked you if you were OK, you said yes, and he fixed the lock. Done what he was supposed to do, end of story. Of course, that's a mismatch to what you would have wanted or your attachment system would have needed, but that is not his fault. And it is not yours either; those things are very difficult to put into words right then and there. And sometimes that is just the way it is, we don't always get our needs met", she ended with a kind tone in her voice. "Come on, how about some tea or coffee now?"

"Alright." Kate didn't even bother to ask how Rubber Ducky knew these things. She had long since stopped wondering about her strange little travel companion. Instead, she simply shook herself, as if to get rid of some of the heaviness that had settled into her mind, and made to go to the kitchen downstairs. "Coffee. Hot. Yes please."

The next morning, Kate woke up even before the alarm went off. She had slept reasonably well, although she had to admit that she was looking forward to sleeping in her own bed the night after next. She already knew from the first experience on the ferry that tonight was going to be neither comfortable nor restful, but that could not be helped.

Outside her window, the sky slowly turned from dark to pale light. It promised to be another beautiful sunny day, but this once, she would have preferred rain to match her sadness for having to leave. A few minutes before 6:30am she walked downstairs to the meditation room to meditate with Derek and Stanley for the last time. She was glad that she had decided to join them for morning meditation these past three days. Even though it had meant getting up early, she had felt a sense of calm and peace afterward. Somehow it made for a more balanced way to start the day.

A little while later, everyone was gathered in the kitchen for breakfast: Derek and Stanley, and two other guests. Kate found that she was glad for the company, and thought to herself how odd this was - since she usually liked to be left alone, especially in the mornings before she had had her first cup of coffee. On this trip, however, she had really enjoyed having people around, and had even sought out the company. I wonder if that is a byproduct of being on vacation, or if I am actually getting ready to lower some of my walls, she thought. I suppose time will tell…

She looked around and tried to soak up her surroundings one more time: the wonderful view of the garden from where she was sitting at the breakfast bar, the quiet music in the background, the wonderful smells from the kitchen.

The others began bustling about, getting ready for work, or starting on projects around the house. Soon there was nothing left for her to do either but pack her things, load up the car and get on her way to the ferry.

She said her goodbyes to Derek and Stanley and to the beautiful space that she had been allowed to stay in and, yes, maybe even heal a little more.


The sun shone brightly in a clear blue sky, and the rolling hills seemed to try to add to the color display by shedding the brownish-gray of winter in favor of a fresh spring green. Kate was struck by the stark contrast to the barren, rough and majestic mountains of the Highlands she had seen. Now it seemed as if it had been ages ago when she had walked in those mountains, but she remembered the feeling clearly: the mountains had merely allowed her to be there, just like one might allow a small insect to crawl on the wall because it is inconsequential and it is just too much of a bother to get up and remove it. The Highland mountains were neither inviting nor did they know mercy. One wrong step and you were out.

These hills, on the other hand, were different. More gentle and welcoming.


But even these gentle hills were left behind as the ferry port slowly but unavoidably drew closer.

The arrival at the port, the waiting, the boarding, the stowing the car and getting to her cabin all seemed to pass by in a haze. Kate went through the motions of doing what needed to be done, but felt strangely disconnected from it all.

Eventually, Kate once again found herself standing on the deck alone, bracing against the wind.

The ship began to move with the powerful rumble of the engines below. She watched the land behind her sink into the horizon. Her heart felt as if someone was tearing it to pieces. Tears were streaming down her cheeks, and the strong winds blew them off into the sea. Memories flashed in her mind of all the people she had met and who had in one way or another touched her life, however briefly. She felt an intense mixture of longing, pain, and gratitude. Her fingers gripped the iron railing, unaware of the biting cold. For a while she was unable to move, and stood rooted to the spot, her eyes fixed on the horizon until even the flashes of the light house became dim and then disappeared.

Come on, she told herself. You can't hold on to it. Remember, you have to set free what you love, and maybe it will come back to you. And you made a promise to Loch Lomond that you would be back, remember?

Her body still did not move. It was as if the logical part of her mind had no connection to the muscles. Her heart loathed to go down into the belly of the ship and into her windowless cabin. Even the thought of it felt as if she would be severing the last chord that still connected her to...to freedom, to adventure, to feeling. On this journey, she had been more herself than she had ever been. And now she felt as if she was being led back to prison. As if she had been a bird, allowed to fly free for a little while, and now had to return to her cage. Her soul raged against the arrival on the other side of the

North Sea as if it could already see shackles awaiting her there.

But time has a way of moving on, however desperately we might wish to hold on to it or turn it back. Eventually, the sharp pain changed from a furious inside screaming to a dull numbness. Kate knew this feeling well, she had felt it many times before. It shut off all emotions and thoughts other than those required for the next few steps. In a robot-sort of way, it allowed her to function. Finally, her body responded to commands again and she walked mechanically to the cabin and got herself ready for the night.

When she lay on her cot, the darkness around her matched the darkness inside. There she lay, waiting for the next day to arrive.

Three days had passed since Kate had returned home. The suitcases were unpacked and put away. In a strange way, it was as if she had never been gone, and yet - everything had changed. Even Rubber Ducky was more quiet than usual, as she sat in her usual place by the sink and appeared to be lost in her own memories.

That evening, Kate looked at the pictures she had taken for the first time since she had returned home. Immediately, memories began to flood her mind. She thought about the people she had met, and the connection she had formed with each one. "Isn't in odd, Rubber Ducky", she said, "how we can get so close to someone in such a short span of time? I mean, those conversations I had with Helen or Frances... I told them things I would normally only tell a best friend. Yet it felt good, and right, and somehow fitting. Even though we each knew that within a few days, I would leave and it would be over. And that after I left, the next guest would come, and then the next, and then the next." She was silent for a while. "Whenever I met someone on this trip, I knew from the start that it would not last - but I opened up anyway. And each time, the other person opened up in return, and we shared parts of our stories.

I wonder... I wonder if these intense connections were possible exactly because of these particular conditions. You know, we knew we were only going to see each other for five days, and most likely not ever again. So we had nothing to prove, nothing to expect, and nothing to lose. If they didn't like me, so what? Somehow, this allowed for the freedom to just be me. Which in turn made the connection all the more fun and easy."

Kate sighed. "It is not that easy in real life, at least not for me. The risk seems much greater; I fear to lose people if I do something wrong; I fear they might judge me or not like me anymore. And so I have often stayed silent when I wanted to say something, pulled back when I wanted to be close, or clung to someone who was toxic.

I have loved too much and have been deeply hurt. And I have built a wall around myself after that, and not allowed myself to get close to anyone again. But that is no way to live life, either. Maybe it is time to dare to be me in real life as well. Maybe my fears that *me* is somehow not okay were actually what stood in the way of true connection. Maybe it is time for me to let go of trying to make people like me. Allow those who like me for who I am come into my life and stay, and let the others go; instead of trying to please those that I desperately wanted to stay but who did not want to be part of my life.

I guess that is what it is about in the end, isn't it? Be who you are? Sort through the layers of old fears and patterns and get to the core?"

"I think that comes pretty close", said Rubber Ducky. To be brave enough to step out of your comfortable little box, and find out who you are - out there, in the ring. Or stay inside, where it is comfortable and safe. It is always a choice, I suppose. But," and here she looked at Kate with a wink in her eye, "comfortable and safe is not your thing, not for long anyway. Your soul wants freedom."

"Speaking of", Rubber Ducky continued, "how do you feel now? I mean, before we left, you felt so trapped and paralyzed. Now that we are home again, has that feeling come back?"

"Well…" said Kate thoughtfully. "Yes and no. Remember how at the very beginning, when I stood on the ferry watching the departure, I felt as if I was breaking free and coming home? That has been on my mind a lot. And I think that yes, it was a coming home, but different from what I thought then.

I'm beginning to think that we can never really get away from anything, be it good or bad, because the truth is, those things are not on the outside.

So while I was looking for freedom and a true home some other place, because I thought that the place I was at made me unhappy, it really had nothing to do with the physical location. It had been inside of me this whole time, I just did not see it. It was only by leaving my home and my familiar surroundings, and going to a different country, that I was able to feel it again. At the outset of the journey, I thought that the feeling of coming home came because of Scotland, but I think now that that is not entirely true. I think the truth is that, by leaving behind what I thought was my prison, the connection to my own core, to my home inside myself, was allowed to come to the surface.

And the same thing happened on the way back. I thought that I was going back into prison when I left what I thought was my freedom. But the same way I have home inside of me, I also have prison inside of me. I did not go back into prison. I reconstructed it from the inside. We often don't realize it, but no matter where we go or how fast we run, we take those things with us.

I think there is still so much to understand and to learn from the things I've seen and experienced. The encounters with people on this journey were gifts; gifts that I can use now to work myself out of my prison, and to reconnect with myself."

She stopped and looked sharply at Rubber Ducky. "Is that what you came here for? And why you worked so cleverly to get me to go to Scotland? You knew I needed to get out of here to be able to break out of my rut and be able to see more clearly what is going on. You knew I would not be able to do it if I stayed where I was, because I'd only stay stuck in my analysis paralysis?"

And then, a sudden and surprisingly painful thought hit her: "but you're not leaving now, are you? I mean… your job isn't done yet!" Even while she was saying this, she felt a lump in her throat take shape at the same time as an embarrassed smile played on her lips: she was literally loath to have this small yellow rubber ducky leave her. How bizarre, she thought. Briefly, the memory of the day of the arrival of the envelope and her own very skeptical reaction flashed through her mind. They had been through a lot together in the past weeks, and she had become rather attached to the quirky yet strangely wise creature.

Rubber Ducky smiled her slightly mischievous smile. "Not yet", she said…

FSC
www.fsc.org

MIX

Papier | Fördert
gute Waldnutzung

FSC® C083411

Zeitfracht Medien GmbH
Ferdinand-Jühlke-Straße 7
99095 Erfurt, Deutschland
produktsicherheit@kolibri360.de